Looping to the Limit

Ginney Etherton

This book is a work of fiction. Certain characters are real and their names are used with permission. All other characters, locations, incidents, and dialogue are drawn from the author's imagination or are used fictitiously and not to be construed as real.

For Rich

ACKNOWLEDGMENTS

I owe much to the Bandon Writers Group for their proficient critiques and their unwavering support. Thanks, pals. I would've been a complete mess without you.

Once again, I had the tremendous help of editor L.B. Clark, who is not only skilled and professional, she makes corrections in a way that makes me laugh.

Graphic designer Steven J. Catizone was also with me again. He should get an award for patience and understanding.

Thank you to all of my friends who kept reminding me that I had a book to finish. A special thanks to Christo, my number one motivator.

Chapter 1

"I'M TELLING YOU, boyo. You'd cost your player the hole if you did that in match play," Bushmills was saying when I walked into the shack.

His fabled Irish heritage notwithstanding, Bushmills wasn't in the habit of calling people "boyo," so my eyes searched the room to find his target. They settled on Rocks, who stood against the wall staring down at his Nikes. Two things struck me as unusual right away. One, Rocks had gotten to the caddie shack before I did. And two, he was chagrined.

"You never, EVER, go into the bunker until your player's out." Bushmills gave his audience one of his avuncular chuckles and most charming smiles. Rocks missed the whole thing, but there was a small crowd of Rocks-loathers taking it all in.

"I can tell you, PGA marshals kind of frown on caddies tramping around in the sand before their player has taken his shot. It's called 'testing the surface of the hazard.' Rule 13-4a, if I'm not mistaken."

"I wasn't testing nothing," Rocks protested. "It's just that I was a lot closer than Johnny. Doesn't it make sense that I rake? It wasn't like I was trying to cheat. I didn't say a word to my guy."

Bushmills replied, "Rocks, of course your honesty and integrity aren't in question here, but the officials might not know you like we do."

I giggled without shame, which started the ball rolling for the rest of the guys. They were laughing out loud as I passed by, Rocks only glancing up for a second before focusing on his shoes again.

"What'd I miss?" I asked Tucson Johnny as I plopped myself onto the couch next to him.

"Loads, Lainey," he said. "Catch this. Yesterday, Rocks and I were out together on the Bluffs. Funny thing happened on 12. We each had one player go into the beach on the right side. I was double-bagging, so I hadn't got up to my guy in the bunker yet. You know how that goes."

"Uh-huh," I answered, but I really didn't. I'd vowed to myself, when I first committed to this profession almost a year ago, that I would not get so greedy that I'd risk my health. I do not carry two bags. I will, on a good day, bag for two loops. But only one bag per loop. That's just me.

"Anyway," Johnny continued, "my guy is away, and he blasts out of it before I can catch up. Our hero, Rocks here, says, 'Oh, no problem. I got this.' And he goes ahead and rakes it. Meanwhile, his player is standing there with a WTF look on his face. Now, Bushmills is explaining, in his best Feherty imitation, just how stupid that was."

I nodded. I'd watched that broguish announcer on the Golf Channel. He's funny sometimes, but a little goes a long way. I think Bushmills would take the comparison as an insult.

"You know what, Lainey? I'm startin' to feel sorry for poor ol' Rocksy the Rake. Ever since that ass-chewing Bushmills gave him for sloppy raking last fall, he can't seem to do anything right."

I examined Johnny's face closely. Several scary seconds passed before he cracked a smile and fake-punched my arm.

"Nah. I'm just messin' with you. He's still a dick."

That's what I liked best about Tucson Johnny. He kept me guessing.

The camaraderie with most of the wintering caddies had been tight. I'd call it a brotherhood if it weren't for the fact that they let me in. Except for a couple of weeks during the holidays when the community college was on break, I'd been the only female since the high season ended. Now that we were in the false spring sunshine of February, the tee times had been filling up again and the caddie business had started to look good to enterprising folks, including girls. I ought to know – just a year ago I was one. So a fresh batch of rookies should be stirring things up soon.

What I was really looking forward to was Tiny Sue's arrival. The message I got said she'd left Arizona and had a few stops to make in California before she drove up the coast. I was supposed to be looking for a rental for her. I thought it shouldn't be hard to find a place. Eden Beach always loses people this time of year when the tourist

3

business has dried up and the resident snowbirds are gone. But my connections, bartender/best friend Jessica and landscaper/current squeeze Travis, were no help.

The other caddies might know something, but I couldn't ask them because Sue told me not to tell anyone that she was coming back to work here. I thought that was being overly paranoid, which is rich coming from me, and it was hell keeping the secret. I hadn't heard any trash-talking when Sue left in the middle of summer. At least the serious caddies like Tucson Johnny, Jake, Bushmills, and other good guys knew why she quit the resort to find work as a tour caddie. It's common knowledge that if the female caddies flirt with the male guests, it makes management happy. Tiny Sue was one of the best caddies here, and she didn't need to use her female wiles to give a player a good round of golf. Refusing to do so put her on the bottom of the so-called rotation.

I've followed in her footsteps and, so far, I've gotten by okay. The college girls who bagged in December were flirty, but they're young and that's just their normal behavior. Me being older and wiser at twenty-five, I have more self-respect. And an inability to keep my mouth shut around creeps.

Larson's radio crackle got my attention and I hoped it meant action.

"I need three for a foursome at Hemlock Hollows, pronto." He looked at his clipboard as fifteen caddies salivated like Pavlov dogs.

"Jake, Cheech, and, uh, Lainey. Hop to it."

Yep. I still got it.

MY FIVE-FOOT NOTHIN' frame is burdened with more womanly attributes on top than is reasonable, which has been a nuisance since I turned thirteen. My mom told me, "Just be yourself," and, "If you've got it, flaunt it." She's the best mom in the world, but that conflicting advice has given me more anxiety than solace. I really would rather not be noticed at all. It's just that being myself, a foul-mouthed scrapper with a low threshold for tolerating jerks, seems to raise a lot of eyebrows. Who knows where I would've ended up had I finished college and kept my thoughts to myself. I might've slipped quietly into the conventional world as a degreed jobseeker in debt up to my C-cups.

Instead, I left my hometown in Northern California, headed north, and found adventure on the high seas. Well, after a few less adventurous months waiting tables. And the seas weren't as high as the stupid fisherman I crewed for. But the good part was discovering Eden Beach, the comfy little town on the Southern Oregon coast where I settled. The town doesn't have much going for it in the way of employment, or nightlife, or culture, or social interaction for anyone under fifty. But the scenery is great.

Then there's Singing Bluffs Resort, the thirty-six-hole, walking-only, Scottish links mecca for golfers rich enough to fly here for the best golf experience ever. That's what I hear, anyway. Playing golf doesn't really excite me. The caddie profession, however, does.

Since the invention of the golf bag, there's been the opportunity to pack one for a fee. But it isn't just a matter of hiring on to carry someone's clubs. To me, being a caddie is providing a much bigger service. I'm the best club in the golfer's bag. I'm course technician, statistician, rules referee, tour guide, meteorologist, comrade-in-arms, spiritual guide, and psycho-therapist. I love the game.

Everything except actually playing, that is. I make the claim that you don't have to be a golfer to be a good caddie, though I may be alone in that belief. All the other caddies at the Bluffs play every chance they get. They get out during the empty hours before dark in the worst weather, if management allows. When there's no work they play the muni course, and they'll drive an hour or two to decent nine-hole courses in outlying areas. New guys invite me to join them before they get the staggering news that I don't play. I tried it once and I'm hopeless. Even with Travis's loving encouragement, the thrill did not outweigh the anguish.

For me, guiding the players is the challenge, and spending afternoons in beautiful surroundings with interesting strangers is the reward. Singing Bluffs is a remote resort on the edge of Nowhere, Oregon, so golfers have to be serious enthusiasts to buy into the trip. There is such a buzz, though, about playing these courses so similar to Scotland's in turf, weather, and layout that the hearty keep coming. When I see the expressions on faces of golfers coming off the 18th green, I know I've got the coolest job.

Chapter 2

THE PARKING LOT at Pappy's was half full, normal for a grey weekday afternoon. I spotted Travis's pickup and I smiled. Even though we'd gone way beyond flirting and shy, spontaneous sleep-overs, we clung to our individual lives and didn't check on each other's schedule. But my body reacted with a hot thrill when his tavern time coincided with mine, and with a blue funk when it didn't.

Travis greeted me with his goofy smile before I'd even come though the door. "Hey, how's it goin', Little Lulu?"

I shook my head at the new nickname. Excluding the gross names Rocks called me, I was one of the few caddies at the Bluffs who didn't have a regular nickname. Some were named appropriately, like Spider, Blinky, and Bushmills, of course, who earned his at a pub in Ireland. Others were less obvious, like Cheech, Tick, and Corky, but I learned not to ask too many questions.

Travis and Grant had tagged me with dozens. The knack for pulling funny names out of nowhere was the only thing that the two men in my life had in common. But I don't think they ever knew that about each other. Travis and I were friends when Grant and I were, well, more than friends, and they certainly noticed each other. But I doubt either of them paid attention to the little idiosyncrasies that I found so adorable. Like the way Travis's eyes glazed over behind his rimless glasses whenever his mind latched onto a new idea, whereas Grant's eyes sparkled and the corners crinkled when he smiled. Different, but both cute.

"Little Lulu, huh. Wasn't she a roly-poly cartoon girl with corkscrew hair?" I asked as I climbed onto the barstool next to him.

"Right about the hair, but she wasn't fat. You're confusing her with her boyfriend, Tubby."

"Sure, I am. Because I know so many ancient, obsolete comic strip characters that I get them mixed up."

"Hey, you're the one who bragged about talking with that golfer last year about 'Li'l Abner' characters."

"Enough!" Jessica yelled from behind the bar, setting a pint down in front of me. Beer spilled out onto the coaster and she ignored it. "Gawd, if you two aren't made for each other. This dip-wad," she said, pointing to Travis, "and his stupid nicknames, and you, Lainey, with your grammy-phone music."

Travis said, "I think you mean gramophone."

I added, "And it's a turntable, not a..."

"Whatever! Jeezus!"

Jessica raised her hands in the air, then lowered them to her spiky, maroon and black punk do. Travis and I mouthed, "Yikes!" to each other as Jessica clomped her Doc Martins down the bar.

From the barstool next to Travis came the soft, rational voice of Twitch, my favorite old-timer in all the world. "You'll have to forgive Jessica. I think it's fair to say she's had a bad day."

"Hi, Twitch. How are you?" I asked.

"I'm doing pretty well. Thanks for asking. And you?"

"I'm fine, too. So what's up with Jess?"

"Nothing she won't get past."

Travis and I waited patiently, looking straight ahead, sipping our beers. There was no rushing this wise, old gentleman.

"There were some problems earlier today," Twitch went on. "Firstly, I think Jessica had a bit of a hangover. She didn't look too well when she came in."

That Twitch made a negative comment about Jessica's looks was remarkable. She must have looked really bad.

"Then a delivery came in at the same time a group of motorcycles pulled up. There was a lot of noise."

Twitch took a miniscule sip from his small glass of beer.

Travis asked, "Did the bikers come in?"

"Yep. Four men and two women. I think that's what they were."

I said, "Poor Jess. No wonder she's stressed out."

"I haven't gotten to the worst part yet." He jerked his thumb over his shoulder. "A truck came with a new jukebox."

We turned to where he'd indicated and saw a glitzy chrome and LED-lit monstrosity against the wall. I don't know how I'd missed it. Lights flashed chaotically but there was no music.

"Did it come with all new CDs?" I asked.

"Not all new, but Jessica was pretty upset that her favorites were missing from the new selections."

"No more Death Cab for Cutie?"

"No, I'm afraid not."

With a concerned tone, Travis asked, "How about Alexisonfire?"

"None."

I said, "Don't tell me Pink is gone."

"Pink is still there," Twitch said, clearly relieved.

I walked over to the jukebox, making sure I gave the pool players, two retired Vets in greasy, green camo caps, plenty of clearance. They ignored me as I poked at the touchscreen. Album covers lit up as I explored selections.

"Wow, there's some good blues on here!" I yelled across the pool table, which didn't faze the players in the slightest. "Champion Jack Dupree...Tab Benoit... "

Twitch said, "I thought you'd like that, Lainey. I noticed that there's even an Ella Fitzgerald album."

I returned to my stool as Travis remarked, "Ella Fitzgerald on the jukebox at Pappy's. What's this world coming to? So how come we're not hearing any music, Twitch?"

"I think there's a mutual agreement to give Jessica a break."

One of the pool players looked up, then back at the table without changing expression.

When Jess walked our way again, I caught her eye.

"Sorry you had such a lousy day, Jess. Too bad about losing your favorite tunes."

"Aw, no biggie." She shrugged and gave us a hint of a smile.

I wasn't sure whether to trust her reaction, but she seemed less pissed off.

"Besides," she added, eyeing the new jukebox, "the delivery guy was hot. I'm pretty sure we're going to have lots of operational malfunctions with this baby."

As soon as her shift ended, Jess headed for home instead of having a beer with us, so I decided that was a good idea for me, too. The high season was still a long way off and my bank account needed to get fatter before I could stop rationing beer money. Travis walked me to my Jeep, ostensibly to say hi to "the dog dude," and I let Rover out. Once their male-bonding romp was taken care of, Travis and I leaned against the fender and did some bonding of our own. Sweet.

Then it was another night at home with just my pooch to keep me warm. Most of the time, that was the way I liked it and I think Rover agreed. He adored Travis, and Grant before him, but he loved me most of all. The little, black mutt and I had been together since I picked him out of a box full of free puppies back in my college days. He'd stuck by me during my many moves, including the homeless period of sleeping in my Jeep and a week on a fishing boat. We may have left our friskier days behind us, but now we were content with our stable life. He'd go with me to Singing Bluffs and hang out in the parking lot, or stay home where he had the run of the neighborhood. I hadn't gotten any serious complaints from my neighbors, and I trusted them to be honest with me. Eden Beach was a small town and I was a relative newcomer. It didn't pay to make enemies.

My little house had everything I needed. The front room had enough "kitchen" to provide for my usual sandwiches or microwaved meals, a thrift store couch, a fish box "coffee table," my treasured stereo and a crate of LPs. The rest of the house included a dinky bathroom, a moldy walk-in closet, and a bedroom just big enough for my double bed.

Such was our happy home. My only complaint was that in the three years we'd lived there, the landlord still hadn't let me paint over the Barbie-Pink door.

Chapter 3

THE PROMISE OF a beautiful day was evident by the 7:00 a.m. sunrise as I pulled into caddie parking. I checked in and saw that early tee times were filled at both courses. All of the requests from guests playing through the weekend went to the seniors, who were already assigned. There were only two rounds scheduled with foursomes who hadn't been assigned caddies. I scanned the room and counted sixteen eager bodies. Not good odds.

Tucson Johnny hustled past me and said, "Come on, Lain. You're with us at the Bluffs."

"What do mean, I'm with you?"

"Bushmills called in. He's dyin' of the flu or something and couldn't make it." He shook his head. "Man, it must be freakin' serious for Bushmills to give up a day. I knew he looked really shitty yesterday, but with his face it's hard to tell."

Johnny went out the door laughing to himself, and I picked up my gear and ran after him, still wondering what was going on. I almost collided with Larson, standing in front of his office door scanning the parking lot.

"Oops, sorry, sir."

"Hey, Tidwell. No problem. Your bus isn't here yet but should be the next one."

He checked something on his clipboard and disappeared back into the office. I joined Tucson Johnny at the curb.

"What's the deal? Why am I going?" I asked him.

"When I heard Bushmills was out, I told Larson to put you in. I knew you'd be here. Larson was still checking the roster and seemed grateful for the suggestion. Problem solved." He grinned at me.

I checked behind me, making sure Larson hadn't changed his mind. Two guys had left the shack and were heading our way. They were both tall and skinny, with hats and sunglasses covering their faces, and hands jammed in the front pockets of their whites. Neither said a word as they stood with us.

Out of curiosity, I smiled and said, "Hey."

It didn't work. Each gave me a quick nod and I still had no clue who they were.

Ever the gentleman, Tucson Johnny said, "Lyle, A.J., you know Lainey?"

One of them said, "Hey," and then I recognized him. I'd seen him at Pappy's, and Travis had called him Lyle. The other one remained silent. Okay, at least I knew who I was dealing with now. Lyle and A.J. were in the too-cool crowd of senior caddies who didn't associate with the likes of me. I originally thought it was because I was a newbie, but now I was thinking it was because I was a girl. They'd not had the opportunity to see me in action, and obviously my inglorious presence in the caddie shack hadn't endeared me to the supercool.

I steeled my resolve to charm their socks off.

The four of us boarded the shuttle and I limbered up by giving the driver a cheery, "Good morning." It was cranky Ruth, who hates cheer of any kind, and the malice my greeting elicited made for an especially hair-raising ride to the Bluffs bag drop. Even Lyle and A.J. exhaled with relief when we came to a stop.

The guest services agent, as the guy at the bag-drop area was called, was new and enthusiastic. He told us his name was Tristan and proceeded to pump our right arms senseless, a performance he repeated with the guests when they arrived. They were young, fit, white, and wealthy, judging by their appearance.

Tucson Johnny sized them up with a gander at their golf bags and said, "Nice sticks."

Tristan introduced me to my assigned player, who told me to call him Mickey. His buddy, staring right at my chest, said, "Mickey, you're such a lucky bastard."

Mickey said, "And you're such a dumbshit. Let's get started."

I picked up his bag and lead the way, calm professionalism oozing from every pore.

Four players and four caddies look like a crowd at the tee boxes, but with an efficient pace of play, it doesn't last long. We moved like a Super Mario video game in the hands of a highly-caffeinated nerd. The four drives were scattered across the fairway, sandwiched between dunes and natural bunkers, and each caddie followed their balls with precision.

Mickey was hitting third. After the away players had taken their shots, we approached his ball.

"What's the distance, caddie?" Mickey asked, pulling a club while still moving.

"A hundred and forty. The pin's in the back third of the green where it slopes to the left."

He didn't question my quick response, so I took it a step further.

"One thing you might consider, sir, is there's about a two-club wind coming right at you."

He held his face to the wind for a moment before saying, "Ah. Duly noted." He exchanged his iron for a longer one.

He made the green, and he got more talkative as we walked on.

"This is my first time here. We're from the valley, Salem and Eugene area, and Dave's the only one who's ever played here before," he said, nodding towards the guy ahead.

"Where do you usually play?" I asked.

"All over, but nowhere like this." His head swiveled to take in the full panorama of seascape, mountains, and forested dunes. Then he boasted, "This is my graduation present. I finally finished my bachelor's at OSU, and this is how we decided to celebrate."

So, as I'd guessed, he was probably a couple of years younger than I was, depending on how long those four years took him.

"What was your major?" I asked.

"Exercise and Sport Science."

Figures.

Dave was the only one who parred the hole. The others weren't used to the hard greens of Singing Bluffs, even though I'd given Mickey a word of warning. For the next eight holes, I continued to wow him, and maybe even Lyle and A.J. Supercool, with my prowess.

At the turn, our players went to get snacks and drinks, and I waited with the other caddies.

Tucson Johnny was lying on the grass under a Doug fir, one of many evergreens left standing by the perceptive course designers.

He grinned up at me and said, "This is about the easiest hundred bucks I've made in awhile. How 'bout you, Lainey?"

"Yeah, it's a good round. These guys play pretty well."

Lyle gave a snort. "They ought to, with that equipment. The bag I'm carryin', the sticks alone are worth more than my car."

"No shit," A.J. said. "Check out the Rolex on my boy. It must be nice to have rich parents."

"At least they've got manners," Johnny said. "I love the country club set. They know how to treat a caddie."

Lyle added, "Yeah, I think even Dumbshit figured out that Lainey can caddie." He grinned at me. "What a shock. A looper who's not only nice to look at, she can read greens."

I smiled, batted my eyes coquettishly, and said, "You bet your sweet ass, baby."

I don't know where I got the chutzpah to say that, but it broke the ice. We stopped laughing and straightened up when we saw our rich kids heading our way. At the 10th tee, Lyle stood next to me while our players waited their turn.

"So, Lainey. You're chummy with Travis, right?"

I wasn't sure where this was going and my answer came out as a question. "Yeah?"

"I was talking to him the other day. He told me you both were interviewed by some golf magazine writer."

Uh-oh. I could picture Travis at the bar, replaying his expansive tour of the new golf course with the sportswriter last fall. Nice for him – he gets to show off his new career as a course architect. But why did he have to mention that she'd interviewed me too? The big dope.

Mickey's turn to tee off saved me from having to reply. The fairway play separated us again, and there wasn't another chance to talk until we left the 10th green and faced the crashing Pacific beyond the bluff tee box at 11.

Lyle caught up with me. He had to yell to be heard over the wind and waves. "Hey, Lainey, you gonna go all big-shot on us when that magazine article comes out?"

I forced a bemused laugh. "No. Are you kidding?" I managed to stop myself from saying, "Don't be silly." That might have given him a big clue that I was anxious about that article. Just not in the way he thought I was.

"What article?" Tucson Johnny asked as he turned to face us.

18

"Tidwell here is going to be makin' headlines. 'First Girl Caddie to Get through a Winter at Singing Bluffs.'"

Tucson Johnny said, "Nah. That was Tiny Sue. She was here a couple of winters, I think."

A.J. picked up on Lyle's tone. "'First Female Caddie to Bust Rocks in the Face.'"

"No, that was Tiny Sue, too," Tucson Johnny said.

"Johnny, we're just fuckin' around. Trying to get a rise out of Tidwell," Lyle told him.

"Oh. I get ya. So, Lainey, what's the story?"

By now, the golfers were lined up and ready. All eyes were on me.

"Nothing. There is no story. I'll tell ya later, Johnny."

Chapter 4

IN A WAY, I guess I should have been flattered that Lyle and A.J. teased me. Like my mom has been telling me since first grade, that means they like me. Yeah, Miss Popularity – that's me.

"So, I don't get it, Lainey. What's the big deal?"

Tucson Johnny and I were walking back the long way to the caddie shack after our loop. Lyle and A.J. had taken the shuttle back because they were itching to get another bag. To me and Johnny, caddying was all about quality, not quantity.

"It's really not a big deal at all," I explained as we walked. "There was this journalist who I bagged for last fall, and she was interested in talking to a caddie about how things worked around here. Because we're a public, Scottish links, walk-only golf resort, it's unusual enough that she wanted to do an in-depth story on it. That's all."

"Sure. That's all. I get it now." He went silent as we matched our strides along the path.

"Except for how did this lady find you? Out of all the caddies in the shack, she just happened on the only ballsy girl in the bunch?"

Johnny's smirk was another thing I liked about him. It called you out on your bullshit and expressed respect at the same time.

"It was a fluke. She got a massage here and the masseuse was a friend, well, actually the daughter of my hairdresser. Well, he isn't really my hairdresser, since, as you can tell, I don't have a hairdresser..."

"Settle, Lainey."

"Okay. Well, that was the connection. This sportswriter questioned me about all sorts of things. I mean, Johnny, she was good! She got me to spill my guts about stuff I had absolutely no intention of saying."

"Like what? Did you make up some crazy stuff? I know I would. Like we've got zombies that come out at night and snatch guests out of their beds. Or that Larson is really an ex-mafioso who's been relocated here by the witness protection program. Or maybe just a simple sex scandal, like Martha in the head office is boffing the..."

"Oh, stop. No, nothing like that. I didn't make anything up. Everything I said was true. Just some of it's not very flattering."

He snorted. "Well, duh. Only a kiss-ass could talk about Singing Bluffs without mentioning some of the crap we have to put up with. So what did you tell her?"

"Well, I remember she asked about how the free-agent thing works, so I told her that we're independent

21

contractors, not like caddies on the payroll in private clubs, that we cover our own taxes and insurance..."

"As if we could afford insurance."

"...and that we have to pay for our own gear and uniforms, that we're charged for services in the caddie shack..."

"Yeah, services. Like water and that shit they call food at the grill. Good. What else?"

"She thought it was weird that there was a disproportionate number of white faces around."

"Yup, that's true. Not exactly an affirmative action program here. Did you tell her about the cockamamie caddie rotation system we've got, that allows management to assign bags indiscriminately? It really burns my ass when a brown-nose doofus like Corky gets a loop while a good A-squad caddie has to sit it out. Like Tiny Sue. They were doing that to her all the time."

"I mentioned that."

"What? To the writer?"

"Yeah." I cringed. "We were talking about how some men act with women caddies. You know, the creeps?"

"Yeah."

"And I wanted to brag Sue up for not playing that game, for being such a professional. Then I kinda let it slip that I thought she was punished for it."

"Oh, yeah. She definitely was. Tiny Sue loved it here. She would never have gone on tour with the rest of the lifers if she'd been given the assignments she deserved."

We'd stopped at the back door of the caddie shack. A couple of smokers were hanging out there but didn't pay us any attention.

"Have you heard from Tiny Sue lately? Does she ever call you or anything? I'd like to know how she's doing."

I couldn't keep the secret any longer. Tucson Johnny was a good guy, and I decided Tiny Sue wouldn't mind.

I smiled and turned so that both of us had our backs to the smokers.

"She's coming back, Johnny. Any day now. But don't tell anyone."

AS SOON AS Rover saw me, he climbed back in the open window of my Jeep and barked. When I got closer, he bounced back and forth from the window to the floorboard of the passenger side. Between barks I heard an unfamiliar bing-bong noise. My cellphone was lying where it had fallen and was evidently trying to tell me something. Since I rarely do anything but talk on it, I was not used to the alert noise it made for a text message. It took me a few tries to remember how to retrieve the text, but I finally broke the code and saw Sue's name pop up.

"Will be in E B Sat. See u after your loop. Pappys."

Saturday. Yikes. I fumbled with some more buttons and sent a reply.

"Good news except I didn't find you a house yet where will you live"

With or without punctuation, I was quite proud of myself. It only took me ten minutes. The bing-bong noise resounded again and I read her reply.

"U gotta couch?"

"OK. C U Sat."

Cute. Just like I knew what I was doing. I was halfway home before the impact of her words hit me. The idea of living with a roommate was alarming. I knew that itinerant caddies shared rentals all the time, but I'd never actually lived with anyone besides my parents. The longest I'd ever had anyone at my house was three days, and that was Grant who I was madly in love with at the time. Not the same as having a pal sleeping on the couch indefinitely. I admired the hell out of Sue, but I didn't think our friendship could survive days of sharing the very small bathroom in my very small house.

I pulled into the shopping center and made for the Laundromat bulletin board. The posted signs were only about lost, found, or free cats and/or dogs. I quickly looked out at the Jeep and checked to see that Rover was still safe. Next, I went into the store and bought the local paper. There were four ads for small, furnished houses or apartments renting for an amount under Tiny Sue's top limit. This was promising.

At home, I called the numbers and jotted down the details of each. Then I phoned Tiny Sue, hoping we'd be able to actually talk instead of leaving messages.

She answered with, "Hey, kid. How's it going?"

"Great, you're there. Hey, I've got a couple of leads on rentals. Want to hear?"

"Okay, yeah, but I'm driving so I can't take notes. Just tell me about them and I'll follow up later if anything sounds good."

"Okay. I don't mind doing any follow-ups, though – whatever I can do to help. It's going to be so cool to have you back in town."

"Yeah, but not breathing down each other's necks. I gotta find my own place, Lainey."

Two amazing minds thinking alike.

Chapter 5

WHEN I TOLD Travis my news, we were burrowed between flannel sheets under the down comforter on his bed. He'd gotten up at first light and fed the fire in the woodstove but the cabin hadn't lost its chill yet. At least that's what his cold body indicated. I hadn't tested it, choosing instead to let him spoil me. I knew if I held out long enough, he'd get up and make coffee next.

I loved staying at his cabin. He kept it clean – a place for everything and everything in its place. Functional furniture, like the bed, was a work of art because he found just the right wood and built it all himself. He'd done such a good job of rebuilding the old place that even in the worst winter storm it was cozy and sound. We'd spent some exciting nights together listening to winds howl like a freight train, but the cabin hadn't lost one shingle. Situated on the back property of his aunt's and uncle's farm on the outskirts of town, Travis's place felt like a secret hideout to me. Whereas when he stayed at my house everyone in town knew about it. Not that I cared, but a girl's gotta have some privacy.

"Okay, where were we?" Travis said, his cold nose nuzzling my neck. "You said you told Johnny about the interview and he thinks it's fantastic. Then, against Sue's wishes, you also told him that she was moving back and was going to caddie at Singing Bluffs again. But there's no secret anymore anyway because she'll be here tomorrow, and you found her a place to rent so it's all good. Right?"

"Right."

"Then, Lainey, why did you give me such a hard time last night?"

"Because! You told Lyle that I talked to that writer. I told you not to tell anyone!"

He sighed, kissed me, and we were through talking. After a while, he got up and made coffee. In spite of our indulgences, our workday started on schedule. Travis left for his office at the new course site the same time Rover and I left for the resort.

The spring-like weather was still holding and the morning at Singing Bluffs was like high season Fridays. There were more guests than on any other day of the week and all of them were excited to get out on the course. I liked to come early, make my way through the lodging areas and see people flitting about everywhere in cars, shuttles, and on foot. Service workers, making their rounds in carts and supply vans, still had enough energy to look like they enjoyed their jobs. Polo-shirted agent types stood in front of the pro shops like car salesmen out in their lots on a sunny day.

The caddie shack, too, was a hotbed of activity. The earliest arrivals were pre-assigned seniors, who had to get there an hour before their tee times, and they kept coming in ten-minute shifts. The rest of us came in when we felt like it, but nothing said "eager" like showing up early, bright-eyed and raring to go. I was back in the bucket again because Bushmills had shown up and was looping for the college kid from yesterday. So I checked in, chatted a few minutes with the other hustlers, then curled up with the Ed McBain paperback I'd found in the Laundromat free box.

I was so enthralled with Bert Kling, the 87th Precinct's dashing young detective, that I didn't notice the level of banter die down when Larson walked in from his office. Blinky, sitting in the chair next to me, poked a finger into my biceps.

"Hey! What's the deal, Blinky? Don't be such a dork."

He squeezed his eyes shut twice in his usual nerdistic manner and said, "Can I read your book while you're gone?"

I blinked back at him in confusion, then heard Larson call me.

"Tidwell, you're fast, right?"

Disregarding the snickers and rude remarks that emanated from the troops, I jumped up and said, "I am."

"I'm making room for a couple of Chamber of Commerce local boys, as a favor. They have push carts but I told them if they sprung for a caddie I'd get 'em on. They've never played Hollows, so guide them along as quickly as you can."

"Yeah, sure. I can do that."

"If they get caught up with the scenery or something, let the group behind you play through."

"No problem, Mr. Larson."

I heard a whiny voice in the background – Corky, I think – say under his breath, "What's she got that I don't got?"

"Finesse, Corky," Larson responded, and abruptly turned back to his office.

I picked up my gear and tossed the paperback to Blinky.

"I want this back so don't get anything disgusting on it. And put it in my Jeep when you leave."

He blinked his acknowledgement.

I walked to Hemlock Hollows bag drop and saw two guys walking up from the parking lot, each tugging a 3-wheeled bag cart. The "boys" were a pair of boomers who I knew to be local realtors. I'd never met them, but I recognized them from the umpteen "For Sale" signs plastered all over town with their cheesy headshots on them. They greeted me and told me to call them Brian and Frank.

We scurried to the first tee to get briefed on the pace-of-play rules, as delivered by speed demon Kelly. We were behind a foursome who looked like low-handicappers, with Spider and Jake double-bagging for them. I was thinking that my twosome would have a hard time keeping up.

Brian, the more jovial of the two, said, "This should be a piece of cake for you today, Lainey. No bags to carry, you can just walk along with your hands in your pockets."

I might have been irked by the insinuation, but he was just too adorable with his chubby-cheeked smile.

"Sounds good to me," I replied. "I guess that means you're going to be leaving your shots right where you want them, avoiding the woods, the tulles, the bunkers covered in beachgrass – and oh yeah, did I mention the elevation change on 13 where you can't see the flagstick from the best approach?"

Frank's eyebrows lifted. "Fat chance," he said, and took out his driver.

He stepped away and took some practice swings.

Brian said, "Okay, okay. You got us. We're gonna need help."

He looked me up and down, the non-confrontational sizing-up I usually get from men over thirty.

Frank said, "The amount of help you need, Brian, you couldn't get from a week at a Leadbetter Academy. If you can keep from losing two sleeves of balls, you'll be lucky."

As usual with men over thirty, I got cocky.

"Well, since I'll have all this time on my hands, I could keep an eye on where your slices end up. It's the least I can do."

They chuckled, I grinned, and we were off to a great start.

After two holes, the guys had lost their jitters and were enjoying themselves. Both had double-bogeyed the first hole and, thanks to my expert greens-reading, bogeyed the par 3 on 2. When we turned eastward and left the ocean views for the woods and meadows of hole 3, the men laughed out loud.

"Are you kidding me?" Frank said. "Is this course under construction, or did they mean to leave all these trees here?"

Brian shook his head. "Outrageous. Forget about losing balls, I would get lost myself out here without a caddie."

"Don't worry about it," I advised. "Pick the right club and line up your shots for accuracy, not distance. It's just another 370-yard par 4. Ignore the landscape. It's here just for looks, something for me to enjoy instead of watching hackers sweat."

I told them the yardage to the first fairway target. As locals, they knew how to feel the effect of the wind without me telling them. Frank pulled his 3-wood and teed up. With a hearty exhalation, he addressed the ball.

He pulled it, but not too badly. His ball hit the hard turf and rolled into the relatively flat part of the left bunker.

"Nice shot," I said. "That's not a bad leave at all. Definitely doable. See, Brian. Nothing to it," I added, trying to keep up the momentum.

Brian got excited and sliced into the woods past the lay-up area.

"Oh, good," I said. "It's nice in there. The rhodies are starting to bloom and they smell great."

By the time we were on the green, the group behind us was waiting to play their approaches. So Brian and Frank holed out and pulled their bag carts to the next tee box as I waved the other group through. When we were at a safe distance but could still see the green, we sat and got out our water bottles. Brian offered me some trail mix, I took a handful and passed the bag to Frank. No one spoke as we munched and watched four balls drop in a shotgun scatter on the green. A breeze was rustling the overhead branches, and unseen birds were singing their little hearts out.

"I'm beginning to see what everyone's been talking about," Frank said. "This course is really something."

"Do you think we'll get out of here with our egos intact?" Brian asked.

Frank shook his head. "When it comes to golf, my ego died a cruel death a long time ago. I'm still keeping score, but I think I won't let it spoil my round. This is just too great."

The foursome were on the green and we watched them putt, with varying degrees of success. They should've had a caddie. They thanked us for letting them play through, and went to the tee box.

Brian said, "When that new course opens, there'll be more golfers coming to Eden Beach than our little town knows what to do with."

"Sell them houses, that's what we'll do," said Frank. "Hey, I just realized. You're Travis's girlfriend, aren't you?"

It was the first time I'd ever heard it put that way, but I guess that's what I was, technically. "Yeah. How did you know?"

"Small town." He shrugged. "That course designer he's working with has got things lined up. I saw on the county website that all the permits had been issued. Everything went through without a hitch and they should be breaking ground soon. Who are they gonna get to do the construction?"

It took me a moment to realize he was asking me. "Do the construction? I wouldn't know. Travis hasn't gone over details like that with me."

Brian laughed. "Yeah, why should she care anyway? They're gonna have carts, not caddies, so what's in it for her?"

Again, his good-natured teasing didn't rile me. I decided that, for real estate agents, these guys were okay.

Chapter 6

PAPPY'S WAS CROWDED by the time I got there. Happy Hour was in full swing and I saw that Jessica was working beyond her shift, helping Curly with the rush at the bar. Travis saw me come in and stood to give me his barstool.

"Hey, Toots," he said, putting his arm around me and leaning in for a discreet kiss. Then I saw who was sitting on the next barstool.

"Sue! Oh, wow."

"Hey, kid."

We hugged and gushed about how good we thought the other one looked while Travis stood grinning down at us. Jessica came over, put a beer on the bar in front of me, and rolled her eyes. Travis pushed some bills across the bar to pay for my beer.

"Thank you, Trav," I said. "I guess you guys met."

"Yeah. Jess introduced us," Travis said. "We've been talking about all the cool courses she's been on."

"It's been a trip," Tiny Sue said. "But it's good to be back in Eden. I must be getting old. I feel like I've come home."

I told her, "You're not old, and you've lasted as a tour caddie longer than I could even imagine doing. How many years has it been?"

"Just four. I know lots of caddies who've been doing it their whole careers. Some of them are in their sixties. What a life, huh?"

Travis spoke up. "How does a guy have any family living like that?"

"Some make it work, either leaving the wife and kids at a home base or packing them along. I've seen guys living in their vans with a wife, babies, dogs, all living like gypsies."

"Wonderful," I said. "I'm thinking those marriages don't last long."

"Exactly," Tiny Sue said. "Most lifers are divorced men, and they've all got a string of girlfriends in every resort area."

Travis said, "What about women caddies?"

"There aren't too many of us. The only ones I've met were caddying because their boyfriends were. Then when they broke up the girl went on to bigger and better things. At least I hope so."

"It sounds like travelling with a circus," I said.

Tiny Sue nodded. "I'm sure you're not far off."

"I guess I can see the allure," Travis said. "There's always the dream of making it big, getting discovered. Like amateur golfers dream of going pro, caddies must dream of getting hired by one."

We drank our beers, and I looked around at the TGIF revelers, most of whom I recognized. Twitch was sitting a few stools down, talking with a little, silver-haired woman I didn't know.

"Who's that with Twitch?" I asked.

"That's Tuffy," Travis answered, puffing his chest with pride. "She's the office coordinator for Azalea Leas Enterprises, an integral part of our design team."

Jessica had come out from behind the bar and joined our conversation.

"Did you say ass-lazies enterprises?" she asked.

"Aw, shit," Travis said, "here she goes."

"Jess, shut up," I told her. "Don't worry, Trav. I'm sure it won't catch on. So, Sue," I continued, "to change the subject, when are you going in to see about getting on the roster?"

"I'm planning on going tomorrow morning. That way I can catch the Artful Dodger at his busiest, surprise him with my entrance." Her eyes took on an evil glint.

"You mean Art Holloway, the caddie director?" Travis asked. "Who calls him 'the Artful Dodger'?"

"Every caddie who isn't kissing his ass."

Travis said, "Really? Do you, Lainey?"

"I don't call him anything. Haven't said anything to him or about him since I started last April. I rarely even see the guy. Sometimes he breezes through the caddie shack, going into Larson's office, but he never stops."

"That's him," said Sue. "He runs things from the titanium palace and doesn't like to mix with the help. Unless you're one of his favorites, one he likes to trade dirty jokes with to impress the high-rollers, he avoids you."

"Ah, I get it," said Travis. "Well, good luck." He tilted his glass to Tiny Sue.

"Thanks. So, tell me more about Azalea Leas."

Travis explained the projected layout and time frame. I'd heard the description before, but each time he told it I got a better feel for the place. It was growing on me.

Tiny Sue said, "It sounds like it's really taking shape."

I agreed, and to show just what kind of supportive girlfriend I was, added, "Who are they getting to do the construction?"

"Andy is hiring a totally local crew, except for Tuffy. She came with Andy because they've worked together a long time and she's indispensable."

"Who's Andy?" Sue asked.

"Andy Mandrake, the course designer from Washington. He's got a number of golf projects under his belt, but this is his first full course. The owners decided to take a chance on him because of his record of conservation, sustainability and efficiency. He's a believer in using available resources, like getting local contractors, and shaping the course around its natural contours as much as possible."

I could see Travis's eyes get that dreamy look that means he's thinking big. His admiration for Andy Mandrake was not news to me, nor was it to Jessica.

"Okay, okay, enough about your hero," she said. "My turn. The jukie guy came in today. His name's Joe."

"Joe the Jukie Guy," I said, nodding. "I like it."

Jessica pulled my attention away from golf course talk with her replay of the forty-five minutes it took Joe to do five minutes of maintenance on the jukebox. If half of what she told me about him were true, he sounded like a decent guy, which would be a first for Jess. I gave her my blessing but advised her not to jump into bed with him just yet. Meanwhile, Travis and Tiny Sue had continued their conversation extolling the virtues of course designs across the country. They were on the verge of covering other continents when I finished my beer.

"Come on, Sue," I said. "If you want to make a good impression on the boss, you shouldn't look like you're living in your car. You're staying the weekend with me, and I go to bed early so let's go."

"Lainey, you found me my own place. Remember? I don't have to stay with you."

"Yes, you do. You can't get the power turned on at your house until Monday. Did you plan on surviving with cold showers and warm blankets?"

"No, I was going to get a motel room."

"Aw, please, Sue. Save your money and sleep on my couch. It's only for three nights. I've got enough groceries to make spaghetti tonight and ..."

"And tomorrow night I'll take you all out for dinner," Travis interjected. "I know Lainey would make you eat her spaghetti three nights in a row and..."

I slugged him.

"...and, though it's good," he said, rubbing his arm, "it's not *that* good."

"Fact," Jessica said.

I slugged her.

Sue sighed in resignation. "Okay, I'll stay, Lainey. But, Travis, you don't have to spring for dinner."

"I want to. Hey, I know. The forecast says sunny again tomorrow, so I'll barbecue at Aunt Gail and Uncle Stewie's house. They'll love it."

"Ooo, a cook-out in February." Jessica's eyes lit up. "I'll bring the s'mores."

I said, "And on the way out there, I'll take Sue past the new golf course."

Travis beamed. "Good plan, Stan." He gave me a quick kiss. To both of us he said, "See you tomorrow. I can't wait to hear how the meeting with Art goes."

Chapter 7

TINY SUE WAS the first lifer back from working the winter-season clubs to the south, and she might've slipped in unnoticed if it hadn't been for Rocks.

"Well, lookey here," he said from his slouch in front of the television when she came in. "If it isn't Smurfette, back from her adventures. Aren't we privileged, to have two ballbusters like Smurfette *and* Sassette amongst our ranks!"

Sue's glare locked on to his face and she slowly shook her head. No one said a word as she continued her stroll through the caddie shack as if it were just another day. Her stare-down wasn't released until she'd crossed the room and reached the chair next to me. Then everyone went back to their previous diversions.

"I see nothing's changed since I left. Rocks is still the moronic dick he always was."

"And always will be," I said. Although I didn't get the Smurf reference, having missed that essential cultural guidance in my childhood, I did know who he meant by "ballbusters."

"Some welcoming, huh?" I put my book down and gestured her closer. "So tell me. How'd it go with Art?"

Sue shrugged and sat down. "Just like I knew it would. I get to his office, he's strutting about like the banty rooster he is, as if the resort would fall apart if he didn't glad-hand every guest personally – like they care who he is. Anyway, I greeted him with all the pizzazz I could muster and he responded with the same good-ol'-boy crap that he does with all the returning caddies he can't remember. You know, like Singing Bluffs is privileged to have you join us...we're more like a family than a team...each and every caddie is an honored member here. But he kept scrunching up his face, like there was a bad taste in his mouth that he couldn't work out."

I asked, "So he doesn't remember putting you on sanctions?"

Tiny Sue laughed. "Nah. Neither did he remember that I was one of the first caddies to sign on here and I've been on the A-list for three years. All he saw was another chick caddie. He told me to check in with Larson and have him add me to the roster."

"I'll bet Larson was glad to see you."

"Yeah. Larson's okay. He doesn't care if you're male or female, as long as you hustle."

She'd hardly finished saying it when the door to his office opened and he grabbed the attention of the room.

"Thurston, you up for a double?"

"You bet." The scrawny guy I knew as "Long Johns" tossed his coffee cup in the trash and he started moving. He was a first-year who'd begun shortly after I had, but we'd never looped together. He got his nickname because, reputedly, he wore nothing under his jumpsuit besides long johns, even in the middle of summer. Ever since I heard that, it's been impossible to shake the image and his proximity made me uncomfortable. Usually, I tried not to think about what caddies have on under their jumpsuits.

"Get to the bus in ten," Larson yelled. "You've got a threesome. So, Tidwell, you."

He called some other assignments, but I was too busy grabbing my stuff to hear them. I felt bad leaving Tiny Sue, but excited to get the bag. She still looked upbeat.

"What are you gonna do?" I asked her.

"Oh, I'll hang here for a few hours, like a well-trained lapdog. You know, so it looks good. Then, after noon or so, I'll take off. I need to go buy a few things for my house."

"'Kay. See you later, then."

"Have a good loop, kiddo."

OUR PLAYERS WERE putting at the practice green near the first tee because play was slow ahead of them. We met them there, and the guest services agent told us they were new to links golf. Long Johns suggested they practice chipping from the fringe to get used to hitting off the firm, sparse fairways they were about to face. They shrugged off the advice, until one of them tried it. The first bounce was within fifteen feet of the hole. The last was ten feet beyond, before the ball ran off the far edge of the green. The three men used the remaining waiting time with their wedges.

42

I thought that lesson would be a good start to earning their respect for the day, but I was wrong. These guys turned out to be the worst kind of hackers. Not only did they have terrible swings, they didn't want course advice from a lowly caddie. These were the kind who give golfers a bad name – loud, arrogant, ill-tempered, and vulgar. My guy told me flat out that when he requested a caddie, he'd made it clear he wanted a girl, one "easy on the eyes" who would laugh at his jokes. The crassness of that mentality was disgusting enough, but he couldn't tell a joke to save his life. I had no trouble not laughing.

I kept wondering whether Larson knew the specifics of the request. If he'd known, why did he pick me? There were two other women in the shack that morning besides me and Tiny Sue. Both were newbies who could only work on weekends and would've welcomed the experience. If Larson knew that this bozo wanted arm-candy instead of a caddie and he stuck me with him, then he was trying to punish somebody. Maybe me, because he saw me talking with Tiny Sue and wanted to warn me not to get cocky. Or Larson got cocky himself and wanted to punish the golfer.

More than likely, he was just following orders. Larson was only the assistant supervisor of caddie services – Art was the big kahuna. I rolled the what-ifs around in my head while I was following Bozo's ball all over the dunes and decided that Larson was still okay. Whether he assigned me for this bag on his own or because Art told him to, it meant Art didn't know me from any other woman in the caddie shack. The guest said he wanted a chick – get him a chick. He might've said to get the short one with the big boobs, for

43

all I knew. The caddie supervisor aimed to please. But he couldn't know that I set higher standards. Larson knew.

I got my only laugh of the whole loop while coming off the front nine. We caught sight of Bushmills and Tick across the dunes on the 13th green, both double bagging. Bushmills signaled us with a questioning thumbs-up. Our players had gone ahead to the port-a-potties, so they didn't see Long Johns set down their bags and point in their direction. He raised both arms high over his head, hands together – the universal sign for dickhead. Chalk one up for the scrawny kid. Bushmills put his hands out in a whadda-ya-gonna-do expression, then tilted an imaginary flask to his lips.

We finished around 3:00 and I couldn't get out of there fast enough. I didn't check the wad of bills the sleazeball had peeled out of his tight little fist, but it wouldn't surprise me if I'd gotten stiffed. Or if I got negative comments on the caddie chit. I wondered how closely Art went over those and reminded myself to ask Tiny Sue if I should worry.

At my Jeep, I found that she'd left me a note scrawled on a Bluffs scorecard, saying that she took Rover. That made me feel good, knowing that she had his company. I phoned her on my way out of the resort and told her I was on my way.

"I'm wrapping it up here, too," she said. "I've got the place all cleaned up and my meager belongings unpacked. I'll see you back at your place in a few."

"Right. First one there gets the first shower. We'll head out to Travis's as soon as we can get cleaned up."

Chapter 8

TINY SUE WAS duly impressed when she saw the worksite at the new course. There wasn't much there yet besides a scratched-out road, a Cat parked on the landing, and an office trailer. I noticed that more gravel had been delivered since I'd last been there.

But Tiny Sue was looking down the valley.

"Incredible. I can already see the first fairway. And the green is in that little saddle over there, about 400 yards out."

"Yeah, that's what Travis told me. How did you know that?" I asked. "All I can see is an old sheep field."

"I've seen so many golf courses, Lainey, I can't drive down the highway without envisioning them on the side of the road. It's a curse. Anyway, this is a beautiful site. Travis is lucky to be in on it, and we're lucky to get to watch. I wasn't here when Singing Bluffs was built."

"I missed it, too. It is kind of exciting, getting in on the ground floor. Travis says we can stop by anytime during construction, as long as we don't get run over."

I whistled for Rover, who was peeing on the tractor treads of the Cat, and we got back in the Jeep. At the ranch, Travis was already at the grill tending the coals. I pulled in next to Jessica's car and one other that I didn't recognize. Stewart greeted me with a big hug.

"Lainey, you're lookin' lovely as ever. What's been keeping you? It's been ages."

I was pretty sure that he and Gail knew whenever I spent the night with Travis – it was impossible to drive past their house without crunching gravel. He was being polite, and I hoped I hadn't hurt their feelings by not stopping by.

"I've just been working, or trying to. Sorry I haven't been in touch."

"Hey, no, don't worry about it. It's good you're here now. And you must be Tiny Sue. Welcome." He waved us forward. "Come on up and meet Gail and Tuffy. I'll go get your beers."

On the porch was the woman who I'd seen sitting next to Twitch at the bar. She and Jessica were leaning back in Adirondack chairs, each with a beer bottle on the arm. Gail came through the kitchen screen door, letting her dog, Angel, out in the process.

"Okay, okay," she told her. "Go see your buddy."

Angel zipped down the steps and around the yard, nipping playfully at Rover and making him spin, trying to keep up.

Tuffy giggled like a kid. It was contagious and our combined laughter gave Angel incentive to circle even faster, until both dogs were coughing from exertion and heading to the water bowl. Tuffy slyly reached into the

46

pocket of her jacket and brought out two dog cookies. It didn't take long for the dogs to recognize the gesture and move into positions of adoration.

As she rewarded them, I introduced Tiny Sue. Gail said, "Hi, Sue. Glad you're here."

Tuffy sprang lightly to her feet. "Well, this must be the Short Girl Club. It's nice to meet fellow members." She gave each of us a steady two-handed clasp.

Sue and I shot each other an amused glance. Tuffy didn't know that we kiddingly referred to ourselves as the Short Grrrls, and Tuffy fit the bill. She was maybe an inch taller than Tiny Sue, with a lean frame but by no means frail. Her blue-grey eyes were still laughing behind her glasses, contrasting sweetly with her rosy cheeks and tidy, silver hair.

"Nice to meet you," I said. "Travis mentioned you to me."

"Oh, and did he mention *you* to me! Yes, I'm afraid you have no secrets any more."

Jessica laughed. "Ha, Lain. You're totally busted."

Travis hollered from the grill, "Tuffy! What are you saying? I did *not* tell her anything, Lainey. She's just a troublemaker."

"Travis, that's no way to talk to your guest," Gail scolded. "Not to mention your boss."

"Oh, that's okay, Gail," Tuffy said. "I am pretty much of a troublemaker. But I'm not his boss."

Travis left his fire-tending to join us on the porch. He gave me a quick hug, then leaned against the railing and

47

said, "No, Tuffy's not the boss. She's the one who tells the boss what to do."

"Well, somebody's got to keep Andy organized. If it weren't for me, that cow field would stay a cow field."

Travis said, "Sheep field."

"Whatever."

Jessica grinned. She was obviously taking a liking to this woman. "What is it you do, Tuffy?"

"Oh, a little of this and a lot of that. I hold the phone a lot, I punch keys, I wave my arms around, and occasionally I take out trash and clean the bathroom. Very grueling, physical labor."

"Which means," Travis said, "she finds and lines up all the right contacts – permit agencies, suppliers, equipment operators, satellite installers, agronomists, you name it. When she's waving her arms, she's directing traffic, either out on the site or in the office because Andy or I have lost something."

Tiny Sue spoke for the first time. "I think it sounds really exciting."

Tuffy patted her arm. "Oh, you poor girl. If you know what's good for you, you'll stick with caddying."

Gail said, "Well, speaking of directing traffic, if Travis would quit holding up the railing, we could get fed sometime tonight."

We all pitched in and got food on the table in a matter of minutes. The sun was dropping behind the hill and the air was cold, but Travis put some wood on the grill's coals to save heat for marshmallows. By the time we finished dinner and gathered around to watch Jessica expertly smash s'mores together, everyone had gotten to know everyone else.

IT WAS LATE when Tiny Sue and I got back to my place, so we went right to bed. But since I wasn't used to snoring sounds coming from my living room – Rover occasionally barked in his sleep but never snored – I lay awake for a while, thinking. I realized how spending time with Gail and Stewart always left me with a feeling of contentment. To me, it looked like they had the perfect marriage.

Once when we were walking our dogs on the beach, I'd asked her whether she missed having kids.

"Not really," she'd replied. "Stewart is kid enough for me. Besides, between us we've got tons of nieces and nephews, and grand-nieces and -nephews, so there's always enough kids around when families get together. No, raising our little herd of cattle, taking care of Angel and the barn cats, and making sure Travis has a good meal once in a while is all the mothering I want to do."

Then we talked about the kids she sees at the grade school.

"There are too many heartbreaking stories, Lainey. I swear, there should be a test that people have to take before they have children. Our dogs get treated better than some of those kids."

I knew Gail volunteered at the school, as well as the community kitchen, and helped organize fundraising efforts regularly. The clearly visible gulf between wealth and poverty in Eden Beach was a topic that came up often on our walks.

"Look at all these designer homes, Lainey," she had said, pointing out the shuttered, sprawling houses that loomed on the bluff. "They stay empty nine months of the year, and there are more of them being built. Yet housing for service-workers, the people who actually live and work here all year, is decreasing."

I said, "I guess you're right. For a community that depends on tourism for its livelihood..."

"Or, even more separated from reality, golf," she added.

"...it doesn't treat its providers very well."

Gail told me, "I know families who are lucky to keep even one wage-earner employed through the winter, or to have a running vehicle. Applications for welfare assistance take time to substantiate and are usually too little, too late. Marriages fall apart...kids get shuffled off to live with relatives...lots of people leave town...and too many resort to crime."

The conversation had then turned to the problem Gail had celebrating the development of yet another luxury-industry business and accepting that her favorite nephew was a big part of it.

"I'm happy for him, Lainey, and very proud," she'd confided in me, with my promise not to tell Travis. "But do we really need another frigging golf course? And right down the road from us! All I can say is, there goes the neighborhood."

"It won't be like Singing Bluffs, though, Gail," I'd said. "It will be more affordable for locals."

I knew that was a weak argument the moment I said it.

"Only locals who can afford an expensive hobby."

"Well, yeah."

She was right, but I felt compelled to find a win-win, a balance between the people I worked around and the people I lived around.

I grasped at the fallback rationale used by developers. "But it will be creating jobs."

"Yeah. For Travis and a handful of construction workers. Then what?"

"Good point. They aren't going to have caddies, and I don't think there's enough room out there for a restaurant or lodging of any kind. They'll need a pro, a course maintenance supervisor, and some groundskeepers. Probably five or six employees. That is pretty sad, isn't it?"

Gail sighed. "Better than nuthin', I guess. And I WILL be hitting them up for lots of fundraiser tournaments. You can count on that."

Chapter 9

THE RAIN RETURNED, faux-spring warmth was over, and it felt like winter again. The caddie shack smelled like wet dogs and dirty feet, their numbers growing. Dirty feet, not dogs, unfortunately.

In one week six boys from the community college had signed on, to try their hand at real-life, as Tucson Johnny put it. Rumor had it that one of the college directors was a drinking buddy of the Artful Dodger, and he wanted an excellent golf team this season. What better way to get an early home field advantage than to walk the courses and watch how others played them? Strings were pulled, and the new caddies were ushered in without prior experience and without taking the night school caddie class.

The way Larson explained it to us, he would pair up a student with a seasoned caddie who would help him learn the ropes. These potential golf champions would learn course management and earn some bucks while they were at it. Singing Bluffs would get some great PR. And the old-timers who were *volunteered* to train the young pups would get some new joke material.

Whatever, I figured that I wouldn't have to work with them because I wasn't "seasoned" enough. They would undoubtedly get sent out with a double-bagger. But my next thought was the realization that they were my competition. *I* was usually paired with a double-bagger. My only shot at getting a bag would be after six other guest-requests for a single bag were filled.

At least Tiny Sue was gaining points because Larson knew what a good teacher she was. She had already looped with each of the students and it looked like she was getting the respect she deserved. They kidded around, calling her "Too Tall" or "Chief," but their tone didn't have any of the sexual innuendos that many dirtbags tried to get away with. Sue told me she was also being noticed by Art.

"You won't believe this, Lainey, but Art passed me in the parking lot and said, 'Good morning.' Like I was a real person."

"Wow. You could be becoming one of his favorites, Sue."

"Oh, hell no. That is not a good thing." She pursed her lips. "If I could only stay under the radar for a little while longer, then I'd have a chance at him."

The menace in her voice had me on the edge of my seat, but before I could get any more out of her, we heard Larson come in. He pointed at her and at one of the students, and they were off. I scowled at the kid as they left, then scowled at the phone in my hand.

Since upgrading from my dummy-phone to the new smartphone that my parents gave me for Christmas, I'd been trying to get the hang of the damn thing in my spare time. I didn't have a computer at home, and I had to admit that peer pressure to dump the previous century was getting to me. After two months I was still fumbling around, using it for little besides phone calls and texts.

"How's it going, Lainey?"

I still had the scowl on my face when I looked up to see Jake taking the seat next to me.

"Whoa. That bad, huh?" he said.

Jake was the best caddie to loop with. He knew everything there was to know about the courses at Singing Bluffs and had a sweet way of giving me pointers without talking down to me. At first, his good looks had made me nervous. But now that I was chatty with his wife at the grocery store where she worked, I could think of him as just a nice guy who happened to be gorgeous.

"Oh, sorry. Don't mind me. I'm just getting tired of losing work to the next best golf team on the south coast."

"Yeah, me too. But it shouldn't last much longer. They'll start their season soon and won't be hanging around here." He nodded at my phone. "You getting anywhere with that thing?"

"Not really. I don't use it that much. Sometimes I even forget to turn it on, or I forget to charge it and it's worthless."

"Let's see."

I handed it to him. "It's evil. I named it Darth."

Jake's finger began swishing faster than I could see as he went through screens I hadn't known were there.

"You checking onto the roster every day like I showed you? You know Larson likes us to use all the bells and whistles available."

"Yeah, I got that down. I can connect to Wi-Fi and check my email, for whatever that's worth. I'm not connected to any social media and don't want to be. Not ready for that yet. Thanks to you, Jessica, and Travis, my tech education is improving. But there are tons of apps on there that I have no use for."

"You want me to get rid of them?"

"Yes! Can you do that?"

"Sure. What about games? Do you want any of these?"

"None. I'm more of a reader than a gamer."

"I noticed. Here, let me show you something." He smiled as he went about making little pictures on the screen disappear.

He fiddled some more then handed it back and pointed to other little pictures. "Go here, then here. Now hold and glide your finger across...you got it. Now you can browse e-zines, music downloads, even read books if you want."

"Hey, thanks, Jake."

"You're welcome. Next lesson, I'll show you how to take a picture of something besides your thumb."

He watched to make sure I could handle it, then left me alone to explore this new dimension. For the next several hours, I checked out websites of some of my favorite musicians, read book reviews, and glanced through golf magazines. I stumbled onto a golfer's blog, then another one, and another one until I realized that everybody and their brother were blogging. Then it occurred to me to Google the sportswriter who had interviewed me.

It felt underhanded, as if I were snooping in her closets. I guess it's done all the time, but I'd never thought of checking out someone I actually knew, and who didn't know I was checking them out. It made me wonder whether people Googled "Lainey Tidwell," but I wasn't curious enough to do it myself. If my name did pop up somewhere on the web, I was pretty sure I was better off not knowing about it.

What I discovered was that Ms. Stannard had a great professional reputation, had received awards for her writing and her photography, had a website and a Facebook page. Seeing that she had opened herself up to that exposure made me feel less like a snoop. She was no different than the musicians I'd been reading about or countless other professionals who seek a following. I would just have to accept the fact that I was in the dwindling minority of people with nothing to shout about.

Chapter 10

TRAVIS AND I had decided to take advantage of a break in the weather and take a walk on the beach. It was cool, but not wet or windy, and the overcast sky was almost the same color as the ocean – slate grey. Usually, I liked the simple beauty of the monochromatic environment, but this time it only indicated approaching doom. I couldn't shake the vision of my name in a magazine that smeared Singing Bluffs,

"Did you read Stannard's article in the *Northwest Golfer* from two years ago?" Travis asked. "It was really good stuff."

"No. I ran out of juice before I got that far."

"You, or your phone?"

"Me. Just my luck one of those college kids had a phone just like mine and charged it up for me. What was the article about?"

"Youth programs. I dug it because it was so clever. She stated the facts, but with just enough bite to get her point across."

"What was her point?" I asked, already suspicious of the word "bite."

"That clubs that didn't have a youth program were pretty bogus. She called them out on it."

I groaned, swore, and fell over a piece of driftwood.

"Lainey! Are you okay? Don't try to get up. You shouldn't put weight on your foot."

Wet sand soaked the seat of my pants where I'd landed, so I did try, and felt stabbing pain in my twisted ankle.

"Well, I can't just sit here. I'll freeze my ass off. I'm okay, just give me a hand."

Rover had scurried over to join the fun, thinking it must be play time since I was down on his level. He licked my face and nipped at my pant legs while Travis tried to take my weight and not trip over him. By the time we were upright and the silly dog was running circles around us, I was laughing between cries of pain.

"Rover, get out of the way!" Travis commanded. "You're really hurt, Lainey. I think you've done a number on your ankle. Come on, lean into me."

He held me against his side as I limped to the truck. I probably looked like an idiot, but his strong arm around me felt wonderful.

"Let's get you home, put some ice on it, and I'll stay with you tonight so you'll keep off it. And you're not going to even try to caddie tomorrow."

"I'll be okay, Trav. There's no need for – *Owww!*"

Without missing a step, Travis swept me up and carried me the rest of the way.

AS STUPID AS I felt for falling on my butt, I relished the special attention from my own personal nurse. He'd put me on the couch with my foot on a pillow and an icepack around the ankle, put Charlie Musslewhite on the stereo, and handed me two Tylenol, a bottle of beer, and a box of Cheez-Its. Then he went to the store to get some real food to fix for dinner. What a guy!

While he was gone I sent text messages to Jessica and Tiny Sue explaining my condition, which caused a flurry of shorthand questions and scrambled replies. I gave it my best shot, but since my fingers were orange with Cheez-It dust and the painkillers hadn't kicked in yet, I decided calling would be quicker. Jessica was still working, so she was quick to grasp that I was not in the ER and said, "Okay. Talk tomorrow."

Tiny Sue expressed more sympathy, but the call was also short. I told her to tell Larson why I wasn't there, that I needed just one day off my feet, and I'd be in the following day. She said she'd explain, told me to take it easy, and we disconnected.

Then I turned my phone off and enjoyed my crackers and blues harp in peace.

When Travis got back, he made chicken and veggie stir-fry over rice and served mine in a bowl. I just had to put the bowl up to my mouth and shovel it in.

"This is really good, Trav. What's in it? It tastes a lot better than any stir-fry I've ever made."

"It's called seasoning, Lainey. You now have salt, cumin, and cayenne on your shelf. I thought that was good for starters. One of these days, we'll get you stocked up and I'll give you some cooking lessons."

He sat next to me and I put my bowl down long enough to get a kiss and a smile.

"I like having a boyfriend who cooks," I said, returning to the food.

After a pause, Travis asked, "What about Grant? Did he cook for you when you went up to Seattle, or did you go to restaurants all the time?"

His tone was without emotion, but he was looking at me with dead-serious eyes. I put the bowl down.

"I dunno. Yeah, I guess he cooked once or twice. I don't really remember."

I put my arm around his back and snuggled into his chest.

"But I do know that no one has ever taken such good care of me. Don't worry about Grant, okay? He doesn't mean anything to me anymore, and he never meant more to me than you do. No one has."

I looked up at the warm, handsome face that I adored, and ran my fingers through his windblown hair. We kissed and he embraced me again.

"I love you so much, Lainey."

"I love you, too. Now, are we good? Do we need to talk more about our past relationships?"

"Nope. What's past is past. Whatever came before made us who we are today. And what we are is made for each other."

He loosened his hold and sat back.

"So, eat up and then I'll help you get showered and ready for bed. We have to get up early enough to get you dressed and out of here by 6:30. You're going to work with me."

Chapter 11

TUFFY HUGGED ME with the fervor of a grandmother welcoming her only granddaughter after a brush with death. With Travis's help, I hobbled up the steps of the office trailer while Tuffy oh-deared to the extreme.

"Oh, you poor thing. Here, let me get you a chair. You'll need this one – it's the best in the house."

She rolled an elaborate ergonomic chair out from behind her desk and held it steady while Travis settled me in.

"Really," I said, "it's not that bad. Just a little sprain."

Travis said, "Yeah, she just needs to take it easy for a while. She'll probably be fine by tomorrow."

I noticed that he was putting a much softer spin on my condition than he'd been advocating all morning. Thank goodness, because I don't think I could have stood two nannies fussing over me.

Tuffy picked up a stool from a drafting table and set it next to her desk. Once she'd hoisted her small frame up to the seat, which she managed smoothly, her knees were even with the top of the desk.

I laughed at the ridiculousness of the situation. "Tuffy, take your chair back. You can't sit like that and expect to work."

"You wanna bet?"

A phone rang from somewhere under the pile of paperwork. She stretched one leg out behind her, balanced with an opposing arm across the desk, pushed things aside and answered it.

"Azalea Leas. Tuffy here."

The grandmother demeanor was instantly replaced with all-business dynamo. She propped her size-five sneakers on the edge of the desk, simultaneously grabbing a laptop and propping it on her knees.

"Travis, make her take her chair back before she breaks her neck."

"Ain't gonna happen. What she says goes around here." He picked up a jumble of documents and tubes from an in-box. "Let me get caught up with a few things and we'll go out on the site. You can drive the buggy for me."

He sat down next to a huge monitor and a weird machine that looked like something from the Starship Enterprise.

"What is that thing?" I asked.

"A CAD printer."

"CAD?"

"Computer-aided design – software for taking data, like the measurements you're going to help me get later, and turning them into drawings. On this."

He patted the machine with affection. Then he got very absorbed in his rolls of documents, and my attention moved to Tuffy. It was fascinating to watch her efficiency, not to mention her balance, but her end of the phone conversation lost me. It consisted of dates, times, and foreign lingo like "mobe," "resource leveling," and "critical chain." Whatever it was she was dealing with, I could tell that she was on top of it.

I looked out the window to see a black Mini Cooper pull up in front of the trailer, and a tall, skinny guy charge out with a big smile on his face. He was fortyish, had seen a lot of sun, and looked good in blue jeans, sweatshirt and ball cap. Behind him, a dusty truck pulled in. The man who got out of it needed every bit of room that huge crew-cab allowed – the driver's half anyway. The other half was taken up by an animal that looked like a gray wolf, only bigger.

Lucky thing I'd left Rover at home.

The truck driver stood motionless, gazing across the valley. He was massive, with a dark complexion and black hair slicked straight back. He had on the same kind of clothes as the skinny guy, but his were well-worn and stained with obvious work-dirt.

"Fantastic," Travis said, rerolling his papers. "Andy's here. And he's got DeSilva. Sweet! Hang tight, Lainey, I'll bring 'em in to meet you."

I got up and followed him out the door. I really didn't want the boss's first impression of me to be the pampered wimp who manipulated his assistant out of her own chair.

64

Travis was approaching the two men in front of the vehicles when they looked up to see me. He came back to offer me a hand but I was already down the steps.

"Lainey, you shouldn't be walking around so much," he said. "Your ankle won't heal if you keep putting weight on it."

The boss walked over to greet me with both arms outstretched. "Ah, so I finally get to meet Lainey, the intrepid caddie. Hi, I'm Andy."

I took it that "intrepid" was a good thing, because although he was more than a foot taller, somehow he put us on equal bearing with the warmth of his two-handed shake.

"Glad to meet your, sir," I said. It was impossible to do anything but smile when looking into this man's face. He wasn't Hollywood handsome, and there was nothing particularly intriguing about him – he was just plain nice to look at.

"I heard you were a great caddie, and I see that you have the professional manners of one. But please call me Andy. What's this about your ankle? Are you injured?"

Travis said, "She sprained her ankle yesterday tripping over..."

"It's nothing terrible," I said quickly. "I'm really fine." I diverted attention away from my ambulatory ineptness by looking past Andy to the man standing off to the side.

"Oh, Lainey, meet Marco DeSilva, our excavator operator. Or, as I like to call him, the Sculptor," Andy said, reaching a sweeping gesture back to the big guy, who exhaled something resembling a chuckle. "Come on over,

Marco. This is Lainey, and I don't think you've had a chance to meet Travis yet."

Travis said, "We've seen each other around. Hey, Marco, how's it goin'?"

DeSilva nodded and said something in a low, deep voice that might've been, "Good."

Andy said, "You'd better let Lobo out, Marco, or Tuffy will kill me."

Lobo. Of course. What else would it be?

Marco opened the driver-side door and Lobo gave him his full attention but didn't move a muscle. Marco nodded once, and the biggest dog I'd ever seen instantly flew out of the truck. He jounced, cavorted, and sniffed crotches (or in my case, armpits) until Tuffy came outside and said, "Hi, Lobo! Come here, boy. I've got a cookie."

I wouldn't have held out anything smaller than my foot to that beast, but Tuffy offered the tidbit of cookie in two fingers. Lobo sat down and waited until she said, "Get it," then gigantic incisors delicately nibbled it out of her hand without bloodshed. Tuffy ruffled the dog's ears playfully.

Andy shook his head and sighed. "By the time this project's completed, that dog is going to be totally spoiled."

She just laughed, opened the door wide, and called the dog in.

Andy continued, "We were just going to have a look at the section plans, Travis. You don't have to be in on this, so why don't you go out and get those elevations we talked about."

"Just headin' in that direction. I'll be right back with the buggy, Lainey. Wait here."

This time I did wait.

IT WAS FUN helping him shoot elevations. Well, he did the shooting. I held the target, once he'd shown me how to level the rod and aim the prism. He'd set up at a location and I'd drive the "buggy," an oversized golf cart with a pickup bed, to sites he directed via walkie-talkie. It didn't hurt my ankle at all and I felt useful.

"This is a huge help to me, Lainey," Travis said, as he loaded the instrument and tripod at the final setup. "I could never have gotten the precision I wanted if I'd had to do it alone."

"How would you? It seems like a two-person job."

"There's other equipment. I could use a laser level, but it'd be slow and I'd end up having to transfer notes. Most everything is done with a GPS, but we want to get things down to a gnat's ass for fine-tuning the greens. Now, thanks to your help, it's all recorded and I just have to plug it in. I can tweak it to my heart's content."

He leaned over to kiss me and I almost drove into a tree.

Back in the office, he showed me how things worked and found jobs I could do without slowing him down or getting in the way. Towards late afternoon, Tuffy had to run into town for the mail and she returned with deli sandwiches and cold beer. I had been so enthralled with the work that I hadn't realized we'd survived all day on trail mix and water. After Tuffy handed out sandwiches, the four of us found a clear place in the room to settle. We could

67

hear Marco's excavator in the distance, and Travis told me that he rarely took meal breaks. That was too bad, because I would've liked the chance to know him better, but I was relieved that I wouldn't have Lobo's gaze on me while I ate.

Andy opened a bottle and handed it to me. It was the good stuff, an Oregon ale that I could never afford to buy for myself.

"This should hold you for now, Lainey, but make Travis take you out to dinner tonight. You've earned it."

"Thanks. But he gets a pass for now. This will do it for me, and I don't think I'll feel much like going out later."

Travis grinned. "You see how hard we work here? And you thought I was a slacker."

"I never said that!"

"Of course she didn't," Tuffy said. "I think Travis just gets a little defensive because of how the good ol' boys in this town talk. Somehow, hard work gets defined by the amount of grime under your fingernails."

Andy put his beer bottle down with an emphasis that got our attention but didn't spill any beer.

"Exactly! And isn't it funny that, in a twisted way, it's the same kind of elitism we get from established architects. Golf magazines are full of their pompous opinions. Readers are bombarded with old-school myths, like anything 'computer' takes away the personality of the design. What hogwash!"

My mouth was full so I nodded to show support, even though I didn't understand what he was getting excited about. But Travis picked right up on it.

"It shows how little they know about computer-ware," he said matter-of-factly. "Any tool is only as good as the skills of its user."

"And smart designers, like you," Tuffy pointed out, "know when to use which tool."

Andy took up the conversation again. "That's what I keep saying. I've had many an argument, in person and online, but there's a giant misunderstanding in some circles that they can't get past. They think we're lazy cretins who never leave our desks – slaves to our technology."

He drained his beer and wiped his mouth with a sleeve. "Which reminds me, I'd better get out there and help Marco on that swale at 14. Tuffy, did you get a new box of paint?"

"Over there in the corner," she replied.

Travis said, "Andy, I'll run Lainey home and be right back. I want to work on this 7th green some more."

"The seventh already? Man, Travis, you are fast."

Andy shoved two cans of spray paint under one arm and hugged me with the other.

"It was great having you here, Lainey. Come join us again any time."

"Thank you, sir. I will."

"Okay. Take care." He put on his cap and headed for the door.

Tully stopped him. "Hey, boss."

"What?"

"Try not to get your hands dirty."

"Yeah, right."

Chapter 12

IT WAS A FASCINATING day. I learned a little about what goes into designing a golf course, and I learned a lot about Travis.

I'd known he was hardworking and thorough because, on the occasions when I'd driven by his landscaping jobs, I'd seen how he transformed homeowners' derelict yards into showpieces. Watching him work had been one of the turn-ons that first attracted me to him. (Who knew that whacking weeds could be so sexy?) I'd also known how smooth and precise he was with his golf swing and that he never lost his cool under pressure.

But seeing him in action around the job site made me realize how he had turned his skills into his passion. The team functioned so easily together, I had no doubt Andy and Tuffy liked working with Travis and respected his results. I saw firsthand how he tackled every part of the job with energy, enjoying it all. Even Marco and truckers delivering loads of dirt joked with him one minute and followed his orders the next.

I decided that my attitude towards work could use some of that enthusiasm. Making my presence in the caddie shack known to Larson an hour before the first tee times was the first step.

"What are you doing here, Tidwell? I thought you needed some R and R," Larson said as he turned away from the snack bar with coffee cup and clipboard in hand.

"No. It really was no big deal, just a little sprain." I gave him a big smile, hoping to distract him from my posture because I was positive favoring my hurt ankle had caused a permanent lean.

I waved my smartphone at him.

"I'm all checked in, ready to roll whenever you need me." We both glanced around the shack. There were eight other caddies milling about, all appearing as eager as I felt.

"Well, it's gonna be slim pickings this morning. But, you never know," he said, "things may start to hustle. You got time for a cup of coffee anyway."

"Yeah, I guess I do," I said, gesturing to the fry-cook. "Coffee, please, and leave room for cream and sugar."

Larson leaned on the counter while I dolled up the burnt, watered-down coffee enough so that I wouldn't be able to taste it.

"So how'd you hurt your ankle?" he asked. "On a run?"

"No, I don't run."

"On a bike trail, then. You're probably a rider."

"No." I stared into my paper cup.

"Rough-housing with your dog?"

"No."

His voice went flat. "Your boyfriend?"

71

"No! Jeez, Larson. I was just walking on the beach."

I felt my face flush. The fry-cook stopped dumping frozen hash browns on the grill to glance over at me.

"I tripped over a piece of driftwood."

Larson started a slow, reticent chuckle. Then it grew to outright laughter and he walked away shaking his head.

"Hey, Tidwell, how's it goin'?"

Jake was leaning against the window sill behind me. I hadn't noticed his arrival because I was so wrapped up in trying to impress Larson.

"Oh, hi, Jake. I'm doin' okay. I took yesterday off, but I'm ready to work now – if there ever is any. How are things with you?"

"I took some time off yesterday, too. Our house needed some repairs, and someone had to be there to deal with the contractor and the landlord. Marjorie has the most stable job right now, so I stayed home."

"She's getting a lot of hours at the store, I guess. I see her every time I go in."

"Yeah, it doesn't pay a whole lot, but at least it's steady. Not like this gig."

We looked around the shack at Gortex-suited caddies and out the window as daylight revealed a gathering of rain clouds to the west.

Determined to keep my positive outlook, I said, "Well, you know these rich golfers. They love a challenge. There's bound to be a few of them who are foolish enough to brave the elements."

"Speaking of foolish, I heard what you said to Larson about falling down." He laughed, but in a nice way. "You didn't really hurt yourself bad, did you?"

"Nah. I've got my ankle wrapped to remind me not to twist it, but it's fine."

To prove I could still do it, I walked over to a couch. Jake joined me.

"Jake, tell me something," I said. "Am I a freak because I don't play golf? Or run, or work out, or kite-board? Is it a requirement of caddies to be crazed sports-nuts?"

"I don't think so. Look at me – I'm not into any extreme sport."

"You golf," I said.

"Not much. It's too expensive, and I don't have time. Not like these single dudes."

"Yeah, well, I'm starting to feel *singled* out. Is it too much to ask that I just be respected for being a good caddie? Anyway, I think this whole hand-eye coordination thing is way overrated."

"Relax, Tidwell. It's not like you're a klutz on the links. You're very capable, and I, for one, respect your work. Who cares what these other chumps think?"

"I gotta care what Larson thinks. And the Artful Dodger – he loves the caddies who're also good golfers. You know he does."

Jake grimaced and nodded. We watched as two kids from the college team came through the door and were greeted with fist bumps from those nearby, including Larson. I ascertained that the excitement was over a practice round played the previous afternoon with some of

73

the caddies. The noise level in the room increased drastically as the group replayed phenomenal shots they'd played, witnessed, or made up. I'd noticed that whenever the younger set was around there was a lot of chest-thumping from the older males, reliving glory days. It didn't matter how many times the stories had been told.

"You know," I said to Jake, "those boys are nice, but I can't wait till they leave."

"It won't be much longer. Their playing schedule starts soon."

We were quiet again until the caddies scattered and the patter dissolved.

"Okay, back to me," I said. "Maybe I should start double-bagging. That could put me on the favorites list."

"Don't do it, Lainey. I know you're tough enough, but don't knock yourself out if you don't have to. It isn't good, double-bagging."

I raised my eyebrows at him.

He let out a sigh and continued. "I do it for the money. But in the long run, it's not worth the price I have to pay."

"Does your back bother you?"

"Like every night. I'm eating Tylenol like vitamins. But I'm not taking anything stronger. For one thing, I can't afford it, either the prescription kind or the street stuff. For another, just look at these guys."

He gestured across the room. He wasn't indicating anyone in particular, but I knew what he meant. It wasn't high-energy drinks or the snack bar coffee that had certain caddies bouncing in their sneakers every morning.

"And consider this, Lainey. Players who double up don't want a caddie – they want a pack mule. You can't communicate one-on-one, can't give 'em the reads they need, can't do anything to make the round their best round ever. You don't want that. You're a great caddie because of the respect you give the game, and it shows."

That was exactly how I expected Jake to respond, and exactly why I'd brought it up. I didn't really believe I had to double-bag to prove myself, but my confidence had slipped. So I wasn't above fishing for compliments when it needed a boost.

"Well, gotta take off, Lainey. Starting at Bluffs in a few." He got up and gave my shoulders a brotherly pat. "Hope you get a loop," he said, and left.

Yeah, getting a loop – that's the trick. It's pretty damn hard to show my stuff if I can't get out.

I decided against a refill of rot-gut coffee and got up to put the paper cup in the trash. I paced around the shack, stopping here and there to glance out the window, or to feign interest in the Golf Channel or bulletin board notices. My thoughts kept circling around the problem. How could I get more loops and still maintain that respect Jake was talking about? I didn't have the seniority that Tiny Sue had, not to mention the experience. But I needed to stand out. What did I have to offer golfers that would make them remember me, tell all their friends, and put me in demand?

A photo display on the bulletin board caught my eye. It had been there forever but I'd never really given it much attention. There were a couple dozen old snapshots of Singing Bluffs' first course under construction. One showed a guy in bib overalls leaning on the track of an excavator, grinning into the camera. The next photo was of the same guy posed more formally, standing next to a man in slacks and a cardigan who I recognized as the famed course designer.

I thought of the various stages of construction Azalea Leas would go through, and wondered how many pictures Tuffy would take of Andy, Travis, Marco, and Lobo. I'd have to remember to ask her for copies.

The door next to the bulletin board opened and Tiny Sue came in, looking as bored as the rest of us until she saw me.

"Hey, you're back. How's the ankle? Can you work?"

"I could if there were any guests. It looks like it's going to be a slow one."

"Oh, I dunno. I think that storm is going to miss us. Maybe some townies will come out."

"Yeah, great. The ones with bag carts. Maybe they'll let me tag along and I could pay *them* for new joke material."

I glanced out the window and reminded myself of the goal to keep a better attitude.

"At least it's not raining," I added.

Tiny Sue took notice of the photos.

"Amazing, isn't it? Look at this one. Is that the 12th tee?"

The picture she pointed to showed a graded fairway, with no trees, snags, or dunes for hints to its location.

"No, the 14th," I said. "See the way it slopes to the right about eighty yards ahead? Out of camera range over here is where it drops off to the far side of number 8."

"You're right. I can barely tell, but you can see the shape of the ground even in these crummy pictures. You're a natural, Lainey."

I studied the rest of the photos with new interest.

Tiny Sue went on. "Seriously, kid. I've noticed that you have an eye for it – how the changing elements affect movement of the ball. Wind is easy, but figuring in air temps, turf densities, moisture levels, grass cuts – all the things that move the ball after it leaves the club – those are tough."

"I think hanging out with Travis yesterday gave me new insights. I want to learn more about what goes into the whys and wherefores of a layout."

"Golfers dig that, Lainey. Tell 'em the intricacies of how a hole was sculpted, how it became that enticing challenge ahead of them, and they'll eat it up. They'll see you got the savvy to recognize their appreciation of such things."

Appreciation for the subtleties of the course – that's what I had.

Larson came in and gave Tiny Sue the high sign.

"Hey, gotta go'," she said. "Let's meet up at Pappy's later. I want to fill you in on our plan's latest development."

Chapter 13

I DIDN'T HAVE a clue what plan Tiny Sue was talking about, so I went to Pappy's early and got a head start on the drinking. To earn it, I first took Rover to the beach. We walked a mile one way in wet sand and back in dry sand to work the kinks out of my stiff ankle. Sitting around the caddie shack all day wasn't very therapeutic, and I definitely needed to burn some calories. Rover had been in the house all day because I'd expected a storm, and he had a case of cabin fever. So the exercise did us both good.

Jessica was working the bar and it was busy enough for her to top off my glass once or twice – taking care not to contaminate the tap, of course – when no one was looking. Consequently, I had a good buzz going by happy hour.

"Don't expect me to catch up with you when I get off," Jessica told me as she replaced my coaster. It was a good ploy to cover her moving my beer under the tap for a discreet splash. "I have time for one quick one, then I'm going home to get ready for my date."

"I know, I know," I said. "You've got a hot date with Joe the Jukie Guy. You've only mentioned it twenty times."

Twitch, sitting next to me, chuckled softly. "Now, Lainey, you're not the only one who gets to boast about your young man."

"That's right," Jessica said. "It's my turn now. We've had to hear about your sexcapades – first Grant, then Travis – over and over. Give it a rest, girl. "

There were two gentlemen, who I thought were local ranchers or cranberry growers or something like that, leaning against the bar beside me. Their conversation stopped when they heard the word "sexcapades."

I turned to face them. "She is so lying. I do not talk about my sex life in here. Whatever you've heard, it's not true. Besides, if anyone has good sex stories, it's Jess."

They were gaping at us and Twitch was turning red when Tiny Sue came up behind me and said, "Does that mean good stories about sex or stories about good sex?"

Without a pause Jessica said, "Both. What'll it be?"

"A beer and a bump. And get Twitch and Lainey another, please."

Twitch made a move to stand up, saying, "Thank you, Sue, but I think I'll mosey on."

I said, "Aw, Twitch, you stay. I promise to behave and not embarrass you anymore. I won't even have another beer."

Jessica put Tiny Sue's drinks on the bar and began pouring another for Twitch.

"Nah, I'd better be going. You girls need to talk. Here, Sue, take my seat."

"Thank you, Twitch. You're a sweetheart."

"Well, if neither of them wants this, I'll take it," Jessica said, hanging on to the beer she'd just poured. "Curly's here so I'm officially off duty and in prep mode for a well-deserved night of hot sex."

She put the full glass on the bar between me and the ranchers. Without a word, they each finished their drinks in one gulp and left.

"Oopsie," I said. "Maybe we were too raunchy for those nice old guys."

"Bullshit," Jessica said. "In case you didn't notice, they were looking at your boobs the whole time they were standing there."

Tiny Sue put money on the bar and took the stool vacated by Twitch. She downed the shot and said, "God, that wind is cold. And it blew in that freakin' big bank of rain clouds that was hanging over the ocean. Did you notice?"

"Nope. I've been in here for two hours."

"Oh. Didn't get a bag today, huh?"

"Nope. Nobody loves me."

"Well, maybe somebody will love you tomorrow," she said.

"Great. It's going to rain like a son-of-a-bitch tomorrow."

Jessica joined us and we drank in silence.

Tiny Sue began again. "On the good side, things are right where we want them as far as our plan goes." She took a sip.

I said, "We have a plan?"

80

"I'm calling it 'Revenge of the Short Grrrls.'"

Jessica said, "O-o-kay then, I'm outta here. Gotta go get gorgeous."

She checked her maroon hair in the mirror behind the bar, finger-spiked it a couple of times, then drained her glass.

"See ya, Jess," I said. "Call me tomorrow. I want details." I turned to Tiny Sue. "Revenge for what?"

"Maybe revenge isn't the right word." She drank, then gave me a sly smile. "Now that I think of it, revolution is better. We could change the female caddie world, Lainey."

"We have a world?"

"Well, the world of Singing Bluffs Resort, anyway. Here, let me see your phone. I want to show you something."

I felt my back pocket and was surprised to find that I had actually remembered to bring my phone with me. I handed it to her and she poked and swiped for a minute.

"There. All set." She handed it back. "See this app, Lainey? I added it to your home screen so it'll be handy."

The unfamiliar logo she pointed to was just one of the many little hieroglyphs on my phone that mystified me. "What does it do?"

"It records. Watch." Tiny Sue poked a button, put the phone in her shirt pocket, and walked down the bar to stand next to where Tick was sitting. It looked like she asked him something but the bar was too noisy for me to hear. Then she nodded and came back to her stool.

She took out the phone again and touched the screen. After looking around a bit, she said, "Get close and listen."

I did, and I heard Tiny Sue's voice say, "How's it goin', Tick? Did you do a dub-dub today?"

It was clearly Tick's voice, low and blunt, answering, "No. Just Bluffs. Two bags, one tip. It's the shits."

Sue's voice again. "I hear ya. I only got one in myself. Well, just thought I'd ask. I'll see ya tomorrow."

I heard a muffled grunt, which was exactly what Tick sounded like when forced to acknowledge someone.

"That's pretty good," I said. "It recorded right through your shirt."

"And if it can pick up Tick at that distance it can pick up anybody. Here, let me show you how to delete. You'll need to practice – you know, to get smooth with it – and you don't want any incriminating evidence in case you leave your phone somewhere. I'm not sure this is legal."

"Cool. But wait, who do I want to record?"

"It all depends. We've gotta be ready for anything that sounds promising."

It must've been the beer. My head was fuzzy and I was having trouble following her.

"Hold everything. Incriminating evidence, secret espionage stuff – what the hell are you talking about, Sue?"

"Okay. Remember me telling you last year about Art's little talk he had with me?"

"Yeah, where he tried to persuade you to get frisky with the high-rolling guests?"

"Right. Well, as the season progresses I'm positive that it'll come up again. I've been nuthin' but sweetness since I've come back, and Art's puny brain sees that as how women should be – sweet, compliant, chump-adoring

82

bimbos. Sure as shit, he's about to make his pitch. And this time, I'll be ready for him."

She pointed to my phone.

"With *my* phone?"

"No, dope. With my own phone. I've got the same program." She took a big slug, finishing her beer. She signaled Curly for another. "I've been practicing for days, but haven't got anything good yet. It might not be Art. It might be Larson, or a brown-nosing caddie, or a player who's been given the green light to schtup any girl caddie he wants. It won't be long, though, before Art pimps us."

"Us? Me, too?"

"*Every* female, Lainey. How many times were you hit on last year? And how many times, after making it clear that you weren't interested, did the dude indicate that he was led to believe otherwise?"

"Uh, a few, I guess. But I always thought it was just Rocks giving me shit again."

"No, girl. He's too afraid of you to try that more than once."

"Really? Do you think so?"

"Lainey, here's what I'm saying. Be on the alert for signs that you've been hired to do more than caddie, and get it on record."

"Okay, I guess I can do that. But then what? What are we going to do with a recording once we got it?"

"That's where the real incriminating comes in." She rubbed her hands together. "I want to get evidence that I can use to hold over Art's fat head. He either meets our demands, or we expose him in public. I don't know where yet – maybe the paper, or some business group, or the Caddie Association. I'll have to see what he's most afraid of."

"Okay, I'm starting to get it. Except the demands. What are we demanding?"

"Respect, Lainey. We're just asking to be treated with the respect we deserve, as good caddies and nothing more. When we're looping, we're doing a job and we expect the same kind of professionalism as the guys get. The male caddies, or bartenders or servers or whatever, don't have to fend off hits from the women guests, do they? There's a double standard here. Management lays us women out on the table like slabs of meat."

It occurred to me that Tiny Sue's exuberance was more than a little alcohol-inspired.

"But, Sue, I feel kinda hypocritical. I mean, because of Grant. I *did* have sex with him when he was a guest. Not for money. Or anything *like* that. Well, he did take me out for an expensive dinner, but that wasn't when we had sex. We didn't even kiss. I don't think we did, anyway. When was our first kiss? I don't quite remember, but I know for a fact..."

"Lainey, stop. That was totally different. You guys were in love."

"Yeah. I guess that is different."

"Damn straight. And if you want to fall in love with another stupid golfer then that's your right."

"I don't. Really, Sue, no more off-course hook-ups for me. No hook-ups whatsoever. Except for Travis, but we're

84

in love, as you say, and he's not a stupid golfer. Well, he golfs, but I never caddie for him."

Tiny Sue reached out and held her hand on my arm.

"It's all right, Lain. You've nothing to worry about. You're as good a caddie as me, and one of these days we'll get recognition."

I was about to get up, but when I turned my barstool I saw Travis coming in with a big grin on his face. He whisked something out from under his arm and dropped it on the bar in-between Sue and me.

I focused on the cover of a golf magazine. Pictured was the magnificent panorama of the Bluffs hole No. 14, unmistakable. In the upper right corner was a small inset, a two-inch photo of a white-clad figure dwarfed by the bag of clubs hanging on her back. The profiled body was obviously female, and the face looking into the camera was obviously mine.

Travis said, "Guess what came in the mail today."

Chapter 14

TRAVIS INSISTED ON following me home from the bar and staying the night. My initial freak-out when I saw my photo on the cover had scared him a little. When I'd calmed down enough, I let him read the article to me.

The cover story was titled, "Build It...But Will They Still Come?" The first paragraph started by pointing out what had already been written about Singing Bluffs. It wasn't news that its superior links had caught the golf world's attention and its reputation was growing. But when Ms. Stannard went on to tell how Eden Beach was "adapting to the impact of this new economic force," I got nervous. Her words began as straightforward observations, but my gut told me she was leading up to something, maybe something she got from me. One could read "Eden Beach's slow quirkiness" as an enticement to a relaxing get-away...or as an apt description of Pappy's major clientele.

Remembering how we'd talked that day I bagged for her, how she kept getting that look on her face and then scribbling something on that damn notepad, made me crazy. No matter how hard I tried, I couldn't remember anything I'd said.

The article listed the benefits of adding caddies to the town's population – creating jobs, stimulating economic growth, introducing a more youthful culture to one otherwise out-of-touch. Stannard quoted a townie barista as saying, "There wasn't anyone here between the ages of twenty-one and thirty before the resort came." As Travis read, he indicated the quotes by saying "quote" and "end quote" instead of doing the finger thing, because that's just the kind of guy he was. I let my mind appreciate that while I tried to relax.

Then came the part that tied my stomach in knots.

Stannard reported the stats about caddies at Singing Bluffs – the male/female ratio, the ranks that are hired in the high season, how few stay through the winter. Then she told about meeting me, describing me as "petite, pretty, and surprisingly tough."

Oh boy, that was going to go over really well in the caddie shack. I could just imagine how that *toughness* would be challenged. And I could never wear mascara or lip gloss again. There really wasn't anything I could do about the petiteness.

Her writing ability really showed, though, in how she exposed the undesirable aspects of the resort. Statements she attributed to me came *after* her opinion. It was on her when she wrote that she'd observed male guests treating female caddies crudely. Tiny Sue's line – that girl caddies should react to dirty jokes and innuendos by keeping a straight face...unless it's really funny – was attributed to "overheard near the pro shop."

"When asked how having your course advice disregarded," she wrote, "Tidwell said, 'It bothers *all* of us to be disrespected, to have our skills undervalued. It probably bothers the guys more, though, because they're not as used to it as we are.'"

That wasn't so bad. It wasn't good, though, that the caption under a close-up of me was, "It's a tricky business being a self-employed woman in a male domain."

Stannard's text explained the business end of caddying at Singing Bluffs – how we're paid, how the resort charged us for "uniforms" and shack services, and how we're responsible for our own income taxes, Social Security and Medicare payments, unemployment insurance, and health coverage.

I was quoted again saying, "I don't know how everyone else does it, but since I left home I've kept good records and reported my income. I have to in order to be eligible for the state health plan. Thank goodness for that."

But the final lob at management was all Stannard.

"In my opinion, more open-minded policies and hiring practices would be necessary for this resort to promote itself as a true community asset.

"There is no doubt that the *Boys' Club* of golf is alive and well at Singing Bluffs, not unlike most private courses. For a public course to be rated as 'top notch,' as this one is, any form of sexism or racism should be out of bounds."

I told myself there was no reason to panic. The magazine's focus was regional. Its readership wasn't as big as that of "Golf Digest." It had only just come out and probably wasn't on the racks yet. Most caddies didn't subscribe to magazines, anyway. They mooched the ones that lay around the caddie shack, the ones that Larson left after he was through with them.

"Hey, Travis, do you think Larson's got his mail yet?"

We were in bed with the light on because Travis was still re-reading the article.

"I don't know, and I don't know where he lives. You're not considering stealing his mail, are you, Lainey? You know that's a federal offense?"

"I'm just thinking."

The part that gave Travis a real rush and held him glued to the pages was the last, a glowing report of the development of Azalea Leas. The writer quoted him extoling the social and environmental benefits of links golf. Travis's confidence in the sustainability of responsibly-built courses, and the promises they held for Eden Beach, came across loud and clear. That she'd ended the article on an upbeat note relieved some of my anxiety. I especially liked where she described Travis as "a dynamic, up-and-coming talent."

"Lainey, did you miss the part where Andy said I was 'indispensable' to him?"

"No, I got it."

When Travis finally put the magazine down and turned out the light, he said, "It's a great story. She did a good job, don't you think?"

"Uh-huh."

He rubbed my back and worked on easing my tensed shoulders. "I don't totally understand why you're upset. We're in a big-time golf magazine! They spelled your name right. They put your picture on the cover *and* inside. You look amazing by the way. Did I tell you that?"

"Yes, you said it but how do I know you're not just saying that to get in my pants? I think I look like a dork."

"Aw, come on, Sweetie. Don't worry about it. This article puts you in a good light. Everything you say is right on. You helped Stannard give people insight into what happens behind the scenes. It shows that caddies like you are smart. You stand out as a spokesperson."

"But that's not right, Travis. That's not the way it's supposed to be. Part of the role of the caddie is *not* to stand out."

"SO FAR, SO good," Tiny Sue whispered to me when I came to stand next to her at the snack bar.

It was early Saturday morning and things were just starting to get busy in the caddie shack. She was stirring two packets of non-dairy creamer and one of sugar into a cup of something I could only assume had started out as coffee.

"I got Art's fair-haired Boy Wonder a minute ago telling me that he bets he'll get more loops than any of the 'prick-teasing honeys' this season. Like that's his big goal. Got it all right here." She tapped the top pocket of her coveralls and sipped the concoction in her cup.

"Oh. I thought you were going to tell me that the coast was still clear, that no one's mentioned the magazine yet."

"You should stop worrying about it, Lainey. It's been out for a week and no one's mentioned it yet, so they probably won't. It's no big deal."

"That's easy for you to say. Anyway, who's Art's fair-haired Boy Wonder?" I asked.

"Over there," she tilted her head towards a tan blonde standing at a vending machine. He was using the reflection in the glass to button his coveralls *just so*. "We call him Miami. He winters in Florida and usually isn't back this early. My guess is somebody big was chasing him. He's a real asshat and the Artful Dodger just loves him. You'll see them chummying up together all the time, swapping gross jokes. And watch – he'll get the best assignments just for showin' up."

She made a gross face to show her disgust. It could've been a reaction to Miami or to the coffee – I wasn't sure which.

Then she added, "He actually said, 'I know I'll get more than you anyhow,' and laughed. He knows how the game is played, and that I won't play it. Remarks like that are going to put it out in the open so everybody knows it."

"Okay, good." I tried to get into the drama of our conspiracy, but my heart wasn't in it. I glanced around at what guys sitting around the shack were reading. No one had *the* magazine.

Larson burst out of his office, almost giving me a heart attack.

"Tidwell! Oh, there you are. Good thing you're here. Someone's asking for you."

This was it. This was going to be ten times worse than being sent to the principal's office.

"Do you remember a Chas Reynolds?" he asked. "Says you bagged for him last year, and he's requested you as his caddie for the length of his stay."

Chapter 15

CHAS WOULD BE a welcome relief. No one better to take my mind off my worries.

Jake was the other caddie assigned to the pair of golfers, just like last year, but this time Chas had a different partner with him. We met them at Hemlock Hollows and Chas gave me a tremendous bear hug that was a great pick-me-up, literally.

"Yo, darlin'. Whatchu been up to?"

"Nice to see you again, too, Mr. Reynolds," I said, giggling like a tweenie.

The guest services agent stood by impassively until all improprieties were over, then gave the formal spiel. The other guest, Jamaal Hart, was shorter than Chas but burlier, which was a little like comparing a Humvee to a tank.

"Man, are we lookin' forward to this!" Chas said, "I've been telling Jamaal what a dynamite round I had here last summer."

Jamaal said, "Hey man, I've heard nothing but good about both courses. And now that we're here I gotta say I like what I see. We've already been warming up on the driving range, so we're pumped." He and Chas did the fist bump thing and made noises as if they'd just come out of a huddle.

"Well, let's get up to the curtain," Jake said, "and let Kelly give her little pace-of-play speech. She's a fast talker and no one's ahead of us so you can tee off, pronto. You're first on the course this morning."

"Crazy. Let's do it, dawg." Jamaal said, and the three men tramped ahead. I hoisted Chas's golf bag high on my back and moved my feet as fast as they would go to keep up. Like Jamaal said, this was going to be crazy.

After three holes, they had relaxed enough to take a look around. As we walked to No. 4, Chas was the one who said out loud the phrase I never get tired of hearing.

"God *damn*, this is a beautiful place. I thought the Bluffs had some sights, but this is...this is beyond description."

"I know," I said. "This is my favorite, and this time of year is the best, I think. By high season, everything changes. But right now I love how the rhododendrons and azaleas start coming out, and the tips of the trees are so green."

As we walked through a brushy trail to the next tee, I reached out to hold a low-lying branch.

"This is a hemlock. There are lots of 'em here, thus the name Hemlock Hollows. See the new growth? Pretty, huh?"

He took the branch in one big hand and played with the delicate needles with the other.

"And soft, feathery even," he said, surprised. "Huh. Guess I hadn't noticed before. Seems like the trees I notice most in Portland, where I'm from, are the big leafy kind."

"I'm sure they have hemlocks there, somewhere."

"Yeah, maybe," he said, "but the only hollow I know is Goose Hollow Tavern."

His giant laugh got the attention of Jamaal, who turned to check us out.

"What's goin' on back there? Am I missing something?"

"The trees, man," Chas said. "You missed feeling the trees." He waved the branch he was holding in Jamaal's direction. Jamaal looked at it, and then at the tree nearest to him, a small spruce. Before I could say anything he took hold of a branch with his ungloved hand.

"Yee-ouch! Son of a bitch!" He stuck his hand to his mouth and sucked. "Whatchu tell me to feel the damn tree for?"

"Whoops," I said. "That's a different kind. Sorry."

Chas couldn't prevent himself from doubling over, his great laughter carrying across the fairways.

Jake said, "It'll stop hurting in a minute. That's a spruce. They hurt."

"No shit they hurt," Jamaal said.

"Quit belly-aching, Jamaal," Chas said. "We're havin' the time of our lives, man. Tee up now. You got the honors."

Their game was a joy to watch. Not just because they were funny, but because they were good. Chas excelled in putting, due to his calming trick of playing a song in his head during his set-up. He told me he'd added John Legend and some classic Ray Charles to his mental play list, occasionally singing them out loud for our entertainment.

They played the course like pros, fast but casual. Both had great swings, with enough power to get down the long fairways and enough control to manage the hazards and the hard turf. The loop was fantastic, and at the end of the day, I had almost forgotten about that stupid magazine article.

THE NEXT MORNING, Chas and Jamaal played the Bluffs and Jake and I met them at the first tee, eager for another great round. On the front nine we were having as much fun as the day before, with both golfers playing hard and laughing harder. They argued about how each hole compared to the holes on Hemlock Hollows, neither able to chose their favorite so far.

When we stopped at the turn stand for a quick break, I looked back and saw another twosome starting at the ninth tee. I recognized the caddie who was packing both bags. It was Miami, and Tiny Sue was right. His body language – the swagger, the cocky tilt of his head with his cap on backwards – read "God's Gift to Golfers" even from a distance.

I got Jake's attention and pointed out the group.

He looked and swore something under his breath. To Chas and Jamaal he said, "We gotta get a move on, gentlemen, so that we don't have to let the following group play through on the next hole."

Our players were finished with their visits to the john, and Chas had started performing some elaborate leg stretches that hurt me even to watch.

"That'd be fine with me," Chas said. "If they wanna high-ball it, they can go right ahead."

"It would be better," Jake said, already picking up Jamaal's bag and readying to move, "if we stay well ahead, if we can. You guys have a pretty fast pace-of-play so I don't see a problem."

I sensed Jake's urgency and got to my feet. Chas let out one last grunt and said, "I'm good to go. How 'bout you, Jamaal?"

"Ready to flow, dawg."

While they were taking a few practice swings at the No. 10 tee box, I quietly asked Jake, "So what's up? Why the push?"

His head reflexively swiveled to look at the turn stand. There wasn't anyone there.

"Well, I'd just rather we didn't have *those* guys on our ass. That's all."

"Why? Who are they? Besides Miami, I mean. I don't recognize the other two. Do you?"

He had to postpone his answer to let our players tee off. Then we were too far apart until we got to the green. The group behind us was already standing at the tee box, looking in our direction.

"Jeez, they got there fast," I said. "No time to even take a pee break."

Jamaal said, "Dudes who don't need to drain the anaconda after nine holes are just askin' for trouble. Packin' all that excess will stunt your growth. You know what I'm sayin'?"

Chas had his putter out and was walking to his ball. He didn't slow his pace, but his deep-throated "Ha-ha-ha" brought gestures of reproach from the tailing golfers anyway. Both had what-the-fuck hands in the air and Miami put the gesture to words, loudly. We weren't even holding them up. There was plenty of fairway for them to take their next strokes.

We ignored them. I told Chas how I thought his lie looked, and Jake took the pin. Neither of our golfers wasted any time with their putts and both of them were in in two. As Jake replaced the pin, Chas waved a come-ahead to the approaching twosome.

"We might as well let these hotheads play through," he said. "They have a fire to get to or somethin', and I sure as hell don't want them breathin' down my neck all afternoon."

I saw Jake mouth, "Oh, shit."

Jamaal was looking back as we moved ourselves and the bags towards the next tee box.

"Yo, Reynolds. You know who that is? Check it out."

Chas looked back then, too.

"Nah. Couldn't be. Ya think?"

"I'm tellin' ya. Check out the pants, man. Ain't nobody with the stones to wear pants like those, 'cept..."

"Holy crap! That's what's-his-name," Chas said. "the guy from ESPN. Isn't it?"

Jake, this time loud enough to be heard 150 yards away, said, "Oh, shit."

I looked again at the guy with the loud pants and his partner, a bulbous waddler with a bad comb-over. Together, they did look familiar, and the mention of ESPN was a big clue.

As resort employees, we are trained (as in, grilled) to not act differently towards celebrities. I actually upheld that rule. Not that I've actually had to, because I hadn't seen one celeb in the almost-one-year I'd been there. I kept hearing about them...Oh yeah, Brad was killin' the front, but he tanked the back...Big Wiesy was here again, did you see her?...I love it when the Blazers are here, don't you?...but I had never seen them. But if I did, I would extend the professional courtesy of not recognizing them.

So, it was to my credit that I didn't show one iota of fanaticism. That, and I didn't really watch ESPN on a regular basis. In other words, who the hell were these guys?

Chapter 16

LETTING SOMEONE PLAY through is a courtesy. As a general rule, recipients show their appreciation with polite thanks and brief patter as they pass the ahead group, then speed up their play to get out of the way as quickly as they can. I've never known golfers to skip this customary routine.

So I got confused when things didn't play out in the normal way. I understood that our players were a little star-struck at first, as if it were their good fortune to step aside and let these famous people pass. Chas and Jamaal were all smiles when the two sportscasters approached the tee box. They threw out compliments for a recent show with enough particulars to prove they were worthy of the same man-cave as these luminaries.

Their flattery was totally ignored. Not only that, but the celebs were taking their sweet-ass time. I waited and listened as they discussed their scores, their choice of club for this drive, the prevailing wind, and how nice the weather was in Hawaii on their last junket. Chas and Jamaal got quiet, and Jake seemed to be grinding his teeth. When Loud-Pants began studying his ball and polishing it with Miami's towel as we watched, I lost control.

"Wow, that ball must be something special. Do you think it's made of a precious material, or does it just have sentimental value?"

I was facing my players and had addressed the question to them, but had raised my voice enough to carry the ten yards to where Loud-Pants was standing. And he knew it. So did Jake, whose jaws had frozen mid-grind.

Chas broke the silence with his signature laugh.

Then he said, "Maybe it was a gift from John Daly...came with the pants."

He scored laughs and a low-five from Jamaal. I smiled big at Loud-Pants to show him that that's how we roll here at Singing Bluffs, that it's our way to have a bit of good-natured fun with guests. I didn't get away with it. The waddler with the comb-over busied himself by lighting up a cigar, and I kept the smile plastered on my face while I had a staring contest with Loud-Pants.

He held his well-polished ball with fingertips and pointed it at me. "You're the one," he said.

Without dropping his gaze, he walked straight towards me until he was an arm's-length away. My mouth kept its smile but my eyes were starting to twitch.

"You're the one," he repeated. "Aren't ya?"

I would've been more afraid if I hadn't been so completely lost.

"The one what, sir?" I asked. "I mean, the one who?" I was suddenly aware that I was holding my weight balanced

101

on the balls of my feet. Although this guy's spit was raining down on me – he was that close – I didn't budge.

"I recognize you from the picture," he said. He turned to his partner. "Figures, doesn't it? Wouldn't ya just know? They give a bitch a good job and she shows her gratitude by shootin' her mouth off."

I felt a rush of energy behind me and Chas stepped between us. He was chest-to-nose with Loud-Pants as he coolly took hold of the situation.

"Whoa now, buddy," he said. "I think you must be mistaking this fine lady with one of yo' stable hoes."

Before I could speak, Jake had me by the arm and was pulling me out of the way, Jamaal was squaring off against Comb-Over, and Miami was falling over golf bags in an effort to back up.

"Hey! Let's keep things moving here. What's the hold-up?" It was the course marshal. He'd driven up in his cart so quietly we hadn't noticed.

"Hi, Bosco," I said, relieved to see it was one of the friendly ones who joked with me all the time. "We're moving. We were just letting these guys play through." I gave Loud-Pants a pleasant smile, as if we'd just been exchanging handshakes instead of glares. "They're in a bigger hurry."

Bosco studied my face for a minute before saying, "Nice."

Then he turned to Miami and said, "Do your job, caddie." Winking at me, he said, "Take it easy, Lainey." And he motored off.

With Jake's usual efficiency and know-how, sides were separated, golf clubs were gathered, and the rounds continued. The worst thing was that I had to put up with the three men gushing over me while we waited for Miami's players to clear the green ahead.

"Okay, can we let it drop? I appreciate everyone rushing to my rescue, but it's really no big deal. He only called me a name, and I've been called a lot worse. And remember, I was kinda the one who started it."

"What? No," Chas said. "You did not start nuthin'. That crazy motha' did it all by hisself. Excuse my language."

Jamaal added, "You got that right. What was he blowin' up about? Recognized you from some picture? Crazy fucker." Then, with a sidelong look at me, "Oh, sorry."

"Never mind! Cuss all you want, you guys. Jake, tell them."

He grinned. "You don't have to watch how you talk around Lainey. If you haven't noticed it by now, she swears worse than I do. And I have no doubt that she could have handled that asshole all by herself. So, Mr. Reynolds, I believe it's your shot."

I TRIED TO keep the ordeal out of my mind for the rest of the round. The guys cooled off and got back into joking, trying to one-up each other with crass insults. But now their insults were directed at the sportscasters and not each other. It was fun, but I couldn't stop worrying about what it meant that Loud-Pants had seen a picture of me.

103

Walking back to the caddie shack after the round, Jake asked me, "You okay, Lainey?"

"Yeah, sure. It was kinda funny, when you think about it. I mean, seriously, how rude can you get? I couldn't believe how those guys walked right past us, not saying diddly about Chas waving them ahead. And Chas and Jamaal were so excited to meet these great sports announcers, like whoo-hoo! They're big, famous talking-heads who sit in a booth and act like they know what they're talking about and..."

"Lainey. It's me, Jake. Don't lie to me. Are you okay?"

"Well, to tell you the truth, I don't know yet."

I slowed my pace and Jake stopped in front of me.

"What? Tell me."

I took a deep breath. "I guess you're gonna find out soon anyway." Then I told him my worst fears, that what I'd said to the magazine writer and she'd put in print was going to come back and bite me in the ass.

"It's not, Lainey. Quit your worrying. You're a good caddie, and that's all you need to know. If the guys upstairs don't see that, then they're crazy. And I know they're not crazy. Just ask Bushmills."

I really wanted to know what he meant by that, but a car horn sounded from the caddie shack parking lot. It was Marjorie, Jake's wife and my friendly cashier at the grocery store. She waved to me and he ran off to get in the car.

I was still muddling over Jake's words when I walked into the caddie shack. It took me a moment to realize that something was different. The troop of caddies who usually slouched around the TV were sitting straight in their chairs.

Instead of the typical non-acknowledgment of anyone entering the room, I was getting quick, repeated glances. I stopped in my tracks and was trying to get my brain to work when Bushmills came up to me.

"This is total bullshit, Lainey. Total bullshit," he said, none too quietly. "There's no way in hell they'll get away with this. Pardon my French."

Chapter 17

"WITH WHAT, BUSHMILLS? Who are you talking about?" I asked, but I had a funny feeling I knew the answer.

"Oh, well," he started, as though he were beginning a story with "once-upon-a-time." "Miami the Muckraker came in here a few minutes ago with the big news flash that you had sullied the good name of Singing Bluffs and all that's holy."

Except for Bushmills, no one else in the room was making a sound. The TVs were muted, and every pair of eyes was on us. Miami was drinking a Coke at the back of the room, and he looked away when he saw me looking at him.

Bushmills continued, "He seems to think, from whatever the blowhards he bagged for told him, that you can be permanently benched."

"Benched? For good? You mean fired? Can that really happen?" My throat was constricting and my voice came out as a high-pitched squeak.

"No," Bushmills said. "No, it cannot happen. Lainey, I don't know who these guys think they are, but they do not...I repeat, do not have the power to take you off the squad. Even if you said half of what they told Miami you said in some magazine, you won't be fired. That just can't happen."

His words sounded more like wishful-thinking than fact, so I clung to his arm for support. Tiny Sue wasn't there, Tucson Johnny wasn't there, and Jake had gone home. Bushmills was all I had.

"Can we go outside for a minute?" I asked him, turning away from what I was sure were accusatory glares from the rest of the caddies.

We went out and sat at a picnic table in the smoking area. Bushmills looked apprehensive, as if I were about to make a WikiLeaks confession.

"What is it, kid? Is everything alright?"

"Yeah, yeah. Everything's fine. It's just that...I don't know where to start. I guess I'm a little shook up."

He began patting his pockets and came up with his tobacco pouch and papers.

"Well, here. Can I get you a smoke? Help you relax?"

"No, thanks, but you feel free," I said. "Before I get into it, tell me something. Jake said something about the guys upstairs not being crazy enough to let a good caddie go, and that I should ask you. What did he mean?"

"Oh, well," he said, his tone suddenly cheerful. "You see, I was one of the first caddies here, before they even opened to the public. The general manager had a couple cronies he was showing around, and I was lucky enough to get assigned to the GM. And for some dumb reason, we just really got along. I guess I did a good enough job because he's been a pal ever since."

Bushmills had finished rolling his cigarette and took a moment to light it before continuing with the story. I liked sitting with him, and it was easy to fall into his level of amusement.

"I'll run into him here and there and we stop and talk. Every once in a while he'll be here with golfing buddies and he'll call me up to loop with 'em. He's really a very good guy. And believe you me, he's saved my butt more than once. Me and the Artful Dodger, we don't exactly see eye to eye, and I probably wouldn't still be around if the GM didn't like me. In fact, he's one of the reasons I keep coming back."

His mood switched again as he looked across the picnic table at me with kind sincerity.

"I don't like to push it too often, Lainey, but if that's what it takes I'll go right to the top for you."

"No, no. I don't want you to have to do that. I'm sure I'm not in that much trouble. At least I don't think I am. Hey, do you know where Tiny Sue is? She knows the whole story and can explain it better than I can."

"I don't know where she is. I've been here since two and she hasn't been around. C'mon, Lainey. Tell me what the problem is."

So I did. My story came out sort of mangled, with partial explanations that led to more explanations that he probably didn't need to know but I found myself saying. His face expressed enough varying emotions to qualify for a Hollywood movie audition. In the end, when I didn't think

I'd left anything out, his face was totally blank. I thought I'd lost him.

But then he said the nicest thing.

"Do not worry, Lainey. Things will fall into place."

ONCE AT HOME with Rover curled up next to me on the couch, a cold beer and a box of Cheez-Its at my fingertips, I tried to let it all sink in. Things were coming at me from too many directions. I wanted to talk to someone who could help me sort it out.

I'd tried Tiny Sue's phone but couldn't think of what message to leave besides "call me."

I knew I could call Travis and he'd be here in a minute. I wanted to. But the problem I was facing...or might be facing, because it was all speculation at this point...was one that needed pure, intellectual analysis without any warm-and-fuzzy, consoling reassurances, no matter how sexy the delivery.

And Jessica, my best friend since the day I'd moved to Eden Beach, was going to be no help at all for this. She just didn't have it in her to understand how caddying, my chosen profession, could possibly mean so much to me.

And that was the issue. Caddying meant something.

Almost everyone I knew who was in their early to mid-twenties had no idea where they would be ten, even five years down the road. It wasn't as if those of us on the rural outskirts of any academia had grown up with a plan. For most of us, college educations were beyond the restraints of our parents' budget and the job market's sustainability was an expensive gamble. The best we thought we could hope for was a decent blue-collar job with benefits. I had to admit that I'd put myself above those women whose only goal was to marry into a better situation, but I knew that sometimes that's all there was.

So when I found my path opening up with the prospect of an authentic, skilled-craft career, it was life-changing. Caddying, for me, was one of those fluke things that you only see in movies, my dream job. I didn't even want to think about what I'd do if I didn't caddie.

My state of mind had deteriorated to a full-blown slump when Darth, my smartphone, sang its familiar song. Thanks to Jessica, "What Does The Fox Say?" stayed in my head for hours after I got a call. It was cute for the first two weeks, but the next time Jess said, "Hey, lemme see your phone for a minute," I was going to have to get mean.

"Hello?"

"Lain, it's me, Sue. I got your message."

"Sue! Where've you been?" I glanced at the clock and saw that it was almost ten.

She made a sound that was half laugh and half tired groan. "Well, it's a long story. But a good one. Actually, it's a great one. But you sound desperate, so you go first. What's up?"

"I'm scared I'm gonna get kicked off the squad, that's what."

"Are you kidding? Don't be ridiculous. You're not going to get kicked off."

"Everybody knows now, Sue. A guy on the course recognized me from the picture in the golf magazine, and he basically told Miami that I was an ungrateful bitch with a big mouth, and Miami told the whole shack."

"Gawd, it would have to be Miami. Who's the guy?"

"I don't know his name, but he's on ESPN. Some sportscaster. But he and his partner were really obnoxious, and I made a joke and it pissed him off. So you gotta figure he went to the managers and reported me, and I'll be fired. I've been thinking about it, and I realize that it doesn't even matter that everything Stannard wrote in that article didn't come from me. People are going to think it was me because I have a big mouth."

"Whoa, whoa, whoa. Slow down. Your mouth isn't that big, and you're not going to be in any trouble."

"How can you be so sure?"

"Because," she paused, making me wait for it, "the recording I now have on my phone is way more damaging than anything Stannard wrote about. Guess who I was out with tonight. You'll never guess."

I heard her laugh again, but this time it sounded more maniacal than tired.

"I'm afraid to guess. Who?"

"The Artful Dodger himself, that's who."

"No way. You mean *out* out? Like on a date?"

"Well, I don't think he would refer to it as a date. More like service in the line of duty. Hey, you know what? I'm seriously wasted, Lainey. I need to get some sleep, and this should wait until tomorrow so you'll get the whole story. Just know that good ol' Art has a way bigger mouth than you, and he's put both feet in it up to the knees."

Chapter 18

SINCE I WASN'T sleeping anyway, I went to the Garden for breakfast as soon as the door opened at six. I sat at the counter with the old guys who meet there every morning for coffee. They were thrilled to have the company of a young woman who wasn't pouring their refills, and especially impressed that I was a caddie. They told some old, corny jokes and I was tempted to tell them some newer ones, but decided against it. These guys were old enough to be my grandpa, and I realized I didn't really know any jokes clean enough for them. So I just gave them what I considered my lady-like smile and ate my number eight over-easy.

Rover hadn't slept well, either, probably sensing my distress, so he had jumped in the Jeep before I left the house. The old guys at the counter had put me in a much better mood and I tried to tell Rover I was going to be okay, that he could stop worrying. It must've gotten through to him because by the time I got to the caddie parking area, he had settled into the passenger seat and looked content. I left a leeward window down for him and told him to have a nice nap.

I had a good feeling that Tiny Sue would greet me with an evil grin and then relate her juicy story about what she had on Art. Whatever it was, it had to be something solid...she had sounded so confident. I could use some of that.

When I opened the door of the caddie shack, the atmosphere inside was heavy enough to knock the wind out of me. In a moment of panic I searched the room for Tiny Sue, but she wasn't in sight. Some of the caddies glanced up and immediately looked away, anywhere but at me, and others snickered and stared.

I stared back with skinny eyes and said, "What?"

Nobody said anything, but when I noticed glances veering towards something behind me I turned around. On the bulletin board next to the door, pinned on top of the ads for cheap rents at affiliated motels and the yellowed Singing Bluffs Rules of Conduct, was my picture. It was the close-up photograph from Stannard's article, but someone had scanned and enlarged it so that it fit on a full sheet of printer paper. As distorted and streaked as it was, there could be no mistaking my face.

Nor could there be any mistaking the crude drawing of a penis at the top of my head.

I felt my jaws tighten and my eyes widen, but I resisted the urge to run. My next reaction had to be good. Any sign of weakness, and, I knew, my opponents would go for the throat.

A hand appeared and yanked down the sheet of paper. It was Rocks. He stepped in front of me and, making a show of it, crumpled the offending picture into a tight ball.

"That's stupid," he said as he walked to the nearest trash can, straightened his arm over it, and opened his hand. The ball of garbage dropped.

Rocks looked at me with his trademark smirk, and I smirked back at him. We nodded to each other knowingly, and turned to face the stunned onlookers. Then we went our separate ways.

After checking in, I took an isolated chair and opened my paperback. Although P. D. James's closed-house mystery with the dashing Superintendent Adam Dalgliesh usually kept me riveted, I couldn't read a word. I told myself no one would notice that I wasn't turning pages. My mind was totally boggled. The fact that Rocks had my back was just plain bizarre. I supposed that meant I had to be nice to him and not refer to him as Rocksy the Rake anymore.

At last, I saw Tiny Sue come in and she headed my way, coolly composed and focused.

"Good, you're sitting by yourself so we can talk," she said as she pulled a chair over to face me.

"Well, I didn't really have a lot of admirers today," I replied. "Someone put a doctored-up picture of me as a dickhead on the bulletin board."

"Probably Miami. He's known for his drawings of dicks...leaves them everywhere. There's one in the men's john with glasses so it looks like Blinky."

"How do you know what's in the men's john?"

114

Before she answered I got back to the issue at hand. "Never mind. It's not important. I want to know what happened last night. Why were you out with Art, of all people?"

She took off her jacket and stuffed it behind her for a pillow. "I might as well get comfortable. I know I won't be interrupted with an assignment today."

I looked at the overabundance of caddies in the room, all of whom had probably not pissed off important guests. "I think I'm in the same boat. But why you?"

"Because the assignments come from Art, and Art is not too happy with me right now. That's why. I dodged the Artful Dodger himself." She grinned. "Remember I told you how he's been nice to me?"

"Yeah."

"Well, I started being nice back, in a perfectly normal way like anyone would be nice to their boss."

"If they had a normal boss," I added.

"Right. Art's not normal. And here's why. Scumbag that he is, he took my good manners to mean that I was courting his favors. You know, givin' some to get some."

"Yuck." I felt queasy from the image that put in my head.

"Don't worry. He didn't get far. The worst part for me was keeping up the innocent act. I almost lost it a few times. He and his icky friends..."

She shivered and made a disgusting, retching sound before continuing. I was bug-eyed but kept silent, not sure I really wanted to hear more.

"I've gotta start at the beginning," she said, in full control now. "Larson put me on Art's bag first thing yesterday morning with these fathead pals of his from Scottsdale. They had girlfriends with them who they said were caddies but really were just big-titted bimbos along for the ride. They didn't know a 3-wood from a 9-iron. The men had their own rickshaws, anyway. But Art wanted to show off, and I was his eye candy."

I laughed out loud. Then it occurred to me she might be serious. My hand went to my mouth and I checked her expression.

"I know. Right?" She laughed, too. "Maybe that means I'm better-looking than that skank Twila...a much better caddie, anyway. Too bad she wasn't there. If she'd have been in the caddie shack that morning maybe she would've gotten the loop."

I said, "I haven't seen her, or that girl she hangs with. I think they're still south."

"Maybe they finally hit pay dirt, found their true sugar-daddies and don't need to work. We can only hope."

I twirled my fingers, urging her to go on. "Okay, so I take it you lasted the whole loop without puking or anything."

"I did, but it was touch-and-go. Then, at the end of a *really* long day, Art says we're going to the club house."

"The club house? You don't mean the den in the basement."

Everyone knew about the VIP members-only man-cave below the lodge. But the only employees who'd seen it were priority servers and housekeeping staff, and they don't talk.

"That's exactly what I mean, and he made it clear that I was invited."

"Get out."

"I'm serious," she said, nodding for emphasis. "He had a driver take me to the shack to clean up and change, and bring me back to the lodge. Luckily, I had my little jacket in my locker. It has inside pockets so I could keep my phone concealed."

Tiny Sue sat back, hands clasped behind her head.

"Man," she said. "I had hoped I'd get Art saying something incriminating, like telling me to flirt more or I'd be benched. But I hadn't dreamed he'd go this far."

"How far?" I asked.

She leaned in and said in a whisper, "He propositioned me."

"What? How?"

"We'd been in the den for about an hour, drinking heavily. The men were playing pool, smoking cigars, drunk on their asses. The girls weren't feeling any pain, either. I'm nursing mine, laughing at their jokes but keeping quiet otherwise. I was worried that my phone's battery was getting low, and I hadn't recorded anything good. I mean, so far it was just the caddie services manager bringing a caddie into the club house. How did I know that hadn't happened before? Maybe he'd only be in a little trouble.

"But just when I'm about to give up and leave, the big dumbass sidles up to me and puts his greasy arm around my back."

"Eew. What did you do?"

"Nothing. I waited. Maybe he took my being quiet for submissiveness, I dunno. Maybe he was stupid drunk. Whatever. But the point is, he actually said, clear as day and loud enough for my phone to pick up, 'How 'bout you and me go find us a vacant room upstairs?'"

Chapter 19

WE DIDN'T EXPECT to hear Larson call out our names, and we didn't. But we were interrupted. Just as I was about to find out how Tiny Sue reacted to Art's come-on, Bushmills marched towards us from the office area.

"Lainey! Just the person I wanted to see," he said. "You'll never guess what I've just been talking about with Larson."

"I'm not guessing anymore. Things are too weird."

He sat next to Tiny Sue, facing me. Sue didn't seem bothered at the interruption – in fact, she looked delighted to see him.

"Hey, guy, come on in and join the party. That is, if you're not afraid that our jinx might rub off on you," she said.

"Afraid? Hell, no. Whatever mojo you ladies have going for yourselves, I'd welcome it."

He had a sprite-like laugh and wrinkled, ruddy cheeks to go with it.

"I mean, you two, even as vertically challenged as you are, have quite the energy out there. When I see you hot-footin' down the fairways like that big bag of clubs on your back is nuthin', I'm duly impressed. If the rest of us mokes followed your lead, we'd be much better off."

Tiny Sue said, "Aw, c'mon, Bushmills. For an old-timer, you're not lookin' too shabby."

"Yeah, but I have to work at it. You two make it look easy."

"Okay," I said, "enough with the BS. You were talking to Larson? Does it involve me? Please say no."

His comeback was quick. "Oh yes, my friend, it involves you to the nth degree."

"What's going on, man?" Sue asked.

"Well, it's like this. I got to thinking after talking with you yesterday, Lainey. And it occurred to me that the best defense is always a good offense."

"Oh, no. What did you do?" I asked, suddenly worried for the three of us.

"I went in to see Mr. Larson this morning, just to shoot the shit. Ya know? Ask his opinion of the new Ping hybrids…you know, just talking. And sure enough, lying on the shelf next to his desk is a copy of *Northwest Golfer.*"

"That must've been where Miami got the picture he ripped off," Tiny Sue said.

Bushmills said, "What?"

"Nothing, nothing," I said. "Finish what you were saying."

"Okay, well, I said to Mr. Larson, 'Boy, that story on the resort is really somethin', isn't it? That Lainey Tidwell sure

120

got this place some good exposure. She should be getting some big pats on the back from the boys upstairs, huh?'"

A whimper escaped my lips. I looked at the two of them, my despair about to skyrocket, but they were both grinning like idiots.

"What'd he say?" Tiny Sue asked.

"Nothing. He sat there staring at me like I was speaking Greek or something. So I said, 'You read it, didn't you? If you haven't, you should. Good stuff. Great PR.' And he said, 'Oh, yeah, yeah, I read it. Yeah, good stuff.' And I said, 'Well, it's nice talkin' with you. I'll let you get back to work,' and that was it."

Tiny Sue let out a laugh and high-fived him. "Excellent!" she said.

"What's so excellent?" I asked. "I don't get it."

"Baby steps, Lainey," Bushmills said. "Baby steps. You just have to plant the seed." He winked at me.

"Right," Sue said. "Now, let me finish my story."

She brought Bushmills up to speed, continuing with how she'd emphatically refused Art's attentions.

"I tried to keep my words clear, but polite. I had to lay it on pretty thick, making sure my actions could not be construed as entrapment. Too bad I didn't have a hidden camera, because he got really pushy. But anyway, he voiced enough threats so that anyone who hears it will get the picture."

"Threats?" I asked.

"Yep. He started with bribes, like telling me he'd make sure I got all the VIPs I could handle, any time I wanted. Then, when he saw that wasn't working, he told me I might

121

as well pack up and hit the road because I wasn't going to carry another bag at Singing Bluffs ever again."

"And you got all that on your phone?" Bushmills looked like he'd just heard his lottery picks announced.

"Yep," Sue answered with obvious pride.

"Man, I want to hear that recording."

"Not here," she said. "Not yet. I'm saving it for something big. I don't know exactly what, or who, yet. I'm still planning my attack."

My stomach roiled. My armpits were dripping sweat, and I couldn't stop my left eye from twitching.

"Hey, you know what?" Bushmills said slowly. "I have an idea."

"I have a stomach ache," I said.

"No. It's simple. What if Sue and I go together? I told you, Lainey, I'd make sure you didn't get benched. Well, now's the time to make good on that promise."

"What are you thinking, Bushmills?" Sue asked.

"I'm pretty tight with the GM, and I'm positive that I can get an appointment. You and I go have a little talk with him, you let him hear that recording, and we tell him how Art's been running things...how he'll run Singing Bluffs right *off* the bluff if he's allowed to continue those shenanigans."

"And that's just the beginning," Sue added. "We can tell him how the public eye is on us now, watching to see if this resort is all it's cracked up to be. We'll give him some insights on how we compare to other new courses...how the image is slipping, leaving Singing Bluffs in the dust."

She sat back with her arms folded and nodded in satisfaction.

Bushmills nodded along with her, and said, "And it took Lainey's interview to bring it all out in the open."

I bolted out of my chair and ran. "Excuse me. I gotta hit the john."

JUST WHEN I TOUGHT I couldn't take any more of the tension in the caddie shack, Mother Nature came to my rescue, dumping buckets of rain, flooding and closing the fairways. Players had to be picked up by service carts and hauled into the lodge. The few caddies who had been out came back in to dry off, get some hot coffee and something to eat. Tucson Johnny was one of them.

"This is the second time since the Bluffs opened that this has happened, and I had to be in on both of them. I shouldn't have ever taken a bag today. It's a real bummer. Now I have to wait for the course superintendents to make the call as to whether players can go back out or not. Hell, anybody with eyesight can see that this storm isn't goin' to let up any time soon."

But for those of us without assignments, we were ninety-five percent sure that no golfer would need our services that day, so we were free to go. My first responsibility was to check on my poor pooch who I'd left in the parking lot. I thought I'd find him curled up in the jeep, drenched from the rain coming sideways through the open window.

I shouldn't have worried. When I finally braved the downpour and ran out to the parking lot, I saw a guest services bus parked next to my jeep. The engine was running, and through the slashing windshield wipers I saw Rover wrapped in a towel sitting on the driver's lap. It was cranky Ruth, and she was smiling. It figured. The only time I'd ever seen her happy, and it took a freak downpour to do it.

She opened the door for me and I climbed into the toasty-warm bus.

"Uh, is everything okay?" I asked.

"Just peachy. Your little feller here looked so alone and scared sittin' in that cold rig of yours, I just had to offer him shelter. Inddat right, lil' buddy?" She gave him a squeeze.

Rover tipped his head up to lick the waddles under her double chins, then looked at me. I read the accusation in his eyes.

"Well, gee, Ruth. That was really nice of you. Thanks for looking out for him."

With some reluctance, she handed him over to me. Of course he was completely dry and water was dripping off my raincoat and hood. Ruth used the towel to dab at the drops that landed on him.

"You should probably get him to a protected spot to do his business," she said. "He's been sharin' my cheese curds and sardines."

"Swell." I looked the little mooch right in the eye, but he was oblivious to any shame. "Okay, well, thanks again, Ruth."

"No problem. Anytime." She smiled and gave a little wave to Rover. "You take care now."

I carried the mutt over to the passenger side of the jeep and rolled up the window. I was dismayed to see my side soaking wet from leaks around the door. I hadn't bothered to put rain pants on, so I used a golf towel on the seat. But with the water dripping from my coat, my butt got wet anyway. I looked over at Rover, his tongue hanging out and an expectant look on his face.

"If you think I'm stopping in a *protected spot* for you, you're crazy. I'm driving straight home and you can just go outside when we get there."

It was treacherous driving, with huge puddles growing faster than the water could drain off the pavement and poor visibility keeping me at a crawl. Finally home, I'd barely gotten into some dry clothes when my phone played Radiohead's "Creep," Jessica's pick for Travis. It wasn't so bad really, if you ignored the lyrics.

I answered with more energy than I felt. "Hi!"

"Hi, sugarlumps. I've been thinking about you, but got too busy to call. Sorry. I hope you weren't out in this. Nasty, huh?"

"Tell me about it. I'm home now. How about you?"

"Just getting ready to leave the site. Everything's really coming along out here, but this storm kinda put the brakes on our plans. So, I'm gonna swing by the cabin and make sure everything's all right, then I was thinking of going to Pappy's. Wanna go? I'll come get you."

"Yes! That sounds perfect. We might as well find some kindred spirits and wait out the storm. And, Trav, plan on making a night of it. I have a lot to tell you."

Chapter 20

THE BEST THING about what Travis and I had going was our mutual empathy. Well, that's not really the *best* thing, obviously, or we wouldn't be falling all over each other every chance we got. Our physical chemistry had to be number one. But right up there near the top was the way we each knew how the other was feeling. I felt there was nothing I couldn't tell Travis or nothing he could tell me that would hurt our relationship.

Not to say that we didn't argue. We had great arguments. Name-calling, sarcastic put-downs, and flipping the bird were all allowed. Just because we could put ourselves in the other's shoes didn't mean they were a style we would've chosen. And every good fight ended with loads of kissing and making up – that physical chemistry thing working again. But ours was not a high-maintenance romance, and the time spent apart, although imperfect, was not miserable. Whenever we reconnected, we always picked up where we'd left off. We were as comfortable as an old married couple – if the old married couple made out like porn stars.

This time, I hadn't seen Travis in four days. We'd talked on the phone Saturday night, but both of us were too tired to get together. So when he came through the Barbie-Pink door to my house, stamping mud off his boots and shaking rain from his hair, I embraced him like he was a sailor home from the seas.

"Hi, doll," he said after the kissing let up. "You're getting all wet. Don't you care?"

Still in his arms, I said, "A little, but it's worth it."

"So, do you want to get naked?"

"Yes, but it will have to wait."

I slithered out of the hug, grabbed a dish towel to dry myself off, and went to get my coat from the closet.

"So if you don't mind, I'd kinda like to go get a beer and talk. A lot has been happening and I'm dying to tell you."

"Okay with me. As long as you don't forget about the getting naked part."

"How could I forget? I think about you naked all the time. I'm doing it right now."

"Nice. But that doesn't count."

I was at the door with Rover waiting impatiently at my feet. I gave Travis the sexiest look I could manage, which wasn't easy to do while wearing an oversized, yellow slicker and a Carhartt cap with ear flaps.

"Later, stud. Let's get going."

"Well, if you insist. But you don't know how hard it is to resist you right now."

PAPPY'S WAS CROWDED, which was the usual situation when severe weather, or even weather with potential, shut down outside work. The fact of the matter, though, is the majority of the clientele weren't working outside. A good percentage of those weren't working anywhere. But whatever, it made for a good crowd in the bars.

Travis and I found Twitch sitting next to Joe, Jessica's new boyfriend. There was one barstool left and Travis pulled it out for me. He took our wet raingear and hung it on hooks next to the door while I ordered beers. Jessica was tending bar, and her attitude and outfit told me she was seriously in love.

"Likin' the look there, Jess," I told her as she set our beers down. Her usual spiked, punked-out do was softened with more brushing than product, and I detected a hint of blue eye shadow behind the heavy black eyeliner. She was also sporting less metal than any biker in the bar, which isn't always the case.

"Yeah, thanks, Lain. Can't say the same for you. You look like shit. How you doin', Travis?"

"Hi, punk," he said, casting a sideways glance at Joe and back at Jess. "Good, good. How you doin'?"

"Oh, I don't know." She slinked over to be face-to-face with Joe. "How do you think I'm doin', Joe?"

She gave him a long, slow blink of her heavily made-up eyelids and smiled sweetly – a side of Jessica that made us all a little uncomfortable.

Joe grinned at her and turned to tell us, "She's hangin' in there."

So much for the niceties.

I tried to hold up my end of the conversation within our little group, but I couldn't think about anything but the pendulum of doom hanging over my head. As much as I wanted to get into the normal routine with by buddies, I so wanted to sit alone with Travis...to talk only about me.

Then Travis said, "Hey, there's an empty booth. C'mon, Lainey, let's grab it. Talk to you later, Twitch...Joe."

Twitch said, "Very good. That's just what you two need. Lainey, don't you worry now. Everything will turn out okay. It always does."

I swear, it's like he and Travis know what I'm thinking and somehow communicate with each other telepathically. I tried not to show my self-consciousness as Travis and I moved from the bar and claimed the booth.

"So, Babycakes, what's going on?"

I breathed in and puffed my cheeks with the exhale. There was a group of women at a table across the room who were partying loudly. Two I recognized from the bank, and two were waitresses at the Garden of Eden.

I asked Travis, "Do you think I'd be any good at waiting tables?"

"No, you're too top-heavy."

I raised an eyebrow at him.

"Seriously," he said. "I've seen women of your stature waiting tables, and their short legs are always running and their boobs are always bouncing. I'm not saying it's a bad thing. I just don't think you'd appreciate the leers you'd get from guys like me. And I know you wouldn't be able to keep your mouth shut, so you'd be fired within a week."

"Yeah. You're probably right. So I guess I'd better tough it out as a caddie."

He put his arm around me so that I had to look him in the eye.

"Lainey, everything was good when we last talked. You got to caddie with Chas again, and you were looking forward to another loop. What happened since Saturday night?"

"Miami put a mean picture of me as a dickhead on the bulletin board." I drank my beer and looked again at the women laughing it up at the other table.

"That's it? Lainey, what's the rest?"

"Well, it all started when Chas and I kinda gave this highfalutin' jerk some flack for slowing down the game, and then the guy says he recognized me from the magazine and he literally stuck his ball in my face. What an asshat. Anyway, then Bushmills tells me not to worry cuz he's friendly with the Bluffs' GM and I won't be fired. So I'm feeling kinda okay, then things got weird when Tiny Sue called and told me she went out with the Artful Dodger."

"Okay," Travis said. "That is definitely weird, but I don't get the relevancy."

"The relevancy is, he thought she would put out for him, and she wouldn't, of course, and he got mad but it doesn't matter because she recorded him on her phone saying all this shit and she's going to hold it over his head."

I drank. Travis waited. I drank again.

"Still not getting it, sweetie. Give me a little more help? Where does the dickhead picture come in?"

"Oh, well, Tiny Sue and Bushmills saw I was upset, and besides that we are all sick and tired of the way Art manages the caddies, so they're teaming up to talk to the GM. About me. About me spilling my guts to the writer about how caddies are treated, which they think is great that I did that but I don't think it's so great, because now the whole shack knows about it and laughed at me when I saw that picture."

"Oh." He finally stopped watching me talk and took a drink. He nodded his head, drank some more, then asked, "What did you do?"

"I just stood there, mortified, afraid to move. Until Rocks came up and ripped it down and threw it in the trash."

"Rocks did?"

"Yeah. Rocks."

"Wow. I guess Miami is the common enemy, making you and Rocks on the same side. Teammates."

He grinned at me.

"That's not funny," I said. "Anyway, I don't know why I have to have a team."

"Well, it sounds like you have one whether you want one or not. Let's see...you have Sue, who doesn't play nice with the guests and secretly records her boss. You've got Bushmills, the old-timer who drinks a little too much but doesn't worry because the GM likes him. And you've got Rocksy the Rake, who's worthless as a caddie and despised by nearly everybody. How could things go wrong?"

I punched him.

131

"Ouch, don't hit me." He laughed while rubbing his arm. "Don't forget, I'm on your team, too, snookums."

Chapter 21

IT RAINED FOR eight days straight, giving my normally sunny disposition and my Gore-Tex jacket a serious workout. The only thing that didn't suck for me was that the plan to confront the general manager about Art was on hold. I was relieved to find out that he was out of town and Bushmills couldn't find out when he was expected to return. So I could relax for a while, but it meant that Bushmills, Tiny Sue, and I were in the same boat as the rest of the mildewed benchwarmers in the caddie shack who weren't on Art's favorites list.

Of those eight days, I showed up to work seven times and got a loop twice. My caddie services for the week brought in barely enough to cover my gas and Laundromat costs, let alone rent and groceries. Travis made sure I didn't go hungry by cooking me dinner at his cabin one night and bringing takeout to my place on another. On my regular Tuesday off, he persuaded me to come out to the Azalea Leas site and see recent progress. I didn't want to disrupt their work, but he said if I came around noon they'd be taking a lunch break anyway, and Tuffy and Andy wanted to see me again. I took Rover this time, thinking that Marco and Lobo wouldn't be out there moving dirt in a monsoon.

I was wrong. Marco's truck was parked in the drive when I got there and there was no sign of the excavator. As I pulled in next to the truck, Lobo's huge head came up from the front seat and scrutinized me like a hungry wolf sizing up an appetizing fawn. I hesitated before opening the door, but Rover had no such reservations and jumped on my lap to get a closer look. Both dogs immediately began wagging their tails and showing toothy grins, so I had to let him have this one.

"Okay," I told him as I let him out, "but you're on your own. I'm not stepping in if you need rescuing, pal."

Tuffy met me on the porch, a hand instantly digging into her pocket for dog cookies.

"Oh, boy! You brought your buddy," she said. "Lobo needs someone to keep him occupied. He's bored with the rest of us."

She went over to the truck and fearlessly let Lobo out. He and Rover sat at attention at the feet of the small woman while she talked baby-talk to them. Side by side, Lobo looked ten times bigger than Rover, but Tuffy had him literally eating out of her hand.

"There's a good boy," she said to each of them. "Now run and play while there's a break in the weather."

She turned to me. "Marco doesn't want him to get muddy, which of course he would if allowed to follow Marco out to the excavation. So I'm the official dog sitter."

"Oh, you are not," Travis said from the office doorway. "You just appointed yourself that so you could come out here and baby that beast instead of working."

"Oh, pooh," she answered. "There isn't anything for me to do in there anyway besides listen to you talk to yourself."

"It's called thinking out loud," he said, walking over and giving me a modest kiss. "Hi, pipsqueak. Come on in. I want to show you this cool terrain model we just worked up."

Usually when Travis wanted to talk to me about the project, he kept to the basics because I'm not interested in the technology of the tools. Sure, I get that the precision is amazing and all that scientific jazz, but how is the hole going to play? What I really liked to hear about was the landscape and how they decided the layout of each hole, especially when it was Travis's brilliance that solved a particular design issue.

So I let him lead me to his work table prepared to make nice and nod appreciatively. When I saw the 3-D image on Travis's computer screen, my eyes popped. Now here was something that explained why he got so excited that he looked high when he talked about his work. Shaping a course with this kind of instrument must make him feel like Captain Picard taking the Starship Enterprise to places where no man has gone before.

"This is hole 8, out beyond this swale to the south," he pointed out by moving the cursor. All at once we were flying and looking down at a switchback fairway to an elevated green.

"Whoa," I said, eyes still popped. "That is amazing."

"I know. Right?"

135

"That's gotta be a par 5. I can see exactly where I'd tell my player to put it."

Travis laughed, and Andy came over from his desk and hugged my shoulders.

"That's what I'm talking about," he said. "It takes a trained eye like Lainey's to see how this hole should be played. That's what I like about you, Lainey. You're more interested in coaching good golf than trying to play it. How've you been? You don't get out here enough. You should bring her more often, Trav."

"I would," Travis said, "but she likes hanging out at that place across town better. Go figure."

"Yeah, well, some days I do," I said. "Not so much lately."

"How *is* business at the Bluffs? Those photos and that great story in *Northwest Golfer* should be getting people's attention. Are things starting to pick up?" Andy asked.

"Not yet, but I guess they will soon. I keep showing up anyway, trying to keep my job."

"Good for you. But please drop by whenever you can. We always need your expert perspective, as well as your charming beauty."

Tuffy had come in and was getting her bag from her desk. "And what am I, chopped liver? Come on, Charming Beauty. Go into town with me and we'll get these con men some lunch."

We put Rover in the car and Lobo back in his truck. It was starting to rain again and he was too big to fit in her car. Tuffy stretched her short legs to floor the throttle and spun tires down the winding, gravel road while I clung to

136

the armrest for dear life. When we got to the main road, she slowed a bit and beamed her lively, steely blue eyes at me.

"We haven't got to talk before, just the two of us," she said. "I'm so glad you're here. And since this is a special occasion, we'll do this up right. Let's buzz into the fish market and get salmon burgers, crab cocktails, some coleslaw...might as well get some ales to go with it. Meanwhile we'll get a few minutes to chat."

I kept my eyes on the road, just in case she missed seeing any oncoming vehicles while chatting.

"Your Travis is such a special guy. I know you know that, but I wanted to tell you how much I admire him," she continued, watching me more than where she was directing the car.

"Yeah," I said. "I guess he is really good at what he does. He seems like a big help to the project. I'm pretty impressed. Yikes!"

Our right front fender nearly clipped the inside bank on a narrow curve as she avoided a cattle truck coming around the other side.

Heedless of my terror, she said, "He has so much talent. Andy couldn't have found a more creative, inspired landscape architect. He's an artist, truly. And just a doll to work with. So expressive!"

She laughed. "You should see when he's concentrating on a particularly troublesome piece...how he pinches at his beard and his glasses seem to fog up. You'd think the top of his head was about to explode."

I had to laugh. "Yeah, I've seen it."

"And then, he gives a sly little smile and, ta-daa! Problem solved."

We got to the fish market in one piece and went in and placed our order. While waiting, Tuffy cheerfully chatted with tourists enjoying their seafood lunches or waiting in line. I watched her work the room as if she were the proud owner. They loved her.

Back in the car for the next leg of Mr. Toad's Wild Ride, Tuffy picked up where our girl-talk had left off.

"But what I really want to say to you about what I admire in Travis, is his maturity."

"Maturity! He makes up silly names for me and gets the giggles when he farts. Tuffy, how is that mature?"

"I know, Lainey, there are times when the boy in every good man just has to come out, for better or worse. But Travis is a planner. And he's always thinking. So I'm telling you this as someone who's been around more than a few blocks. Keep an eye on this mature thinker...he may surprise you."

Chapter 22

I WOKE REFRESHED, all of my rainy-day blues gone. Overnight a new outlook on life had seeped in and taken control. Even the aroma of my morning coffee was invigorating and didn't smell like burnt toast. As I made myself a peanut butter and jam sandwich for the road, I saw the sun rising above the hills outside my kitchen window. The sight reminded me of other mornings when I'd gotten up with a similar lighthearted optimism, making me wonder whether these inexplicable mood swings were normal for people my age. If so, how many new outlooks on life does a girl get? There could be a use-by date when any remaining attitude turnarounds expire and you're left with a pissy mood every morning for the rest of your life.

That thought was so funny I guffawed right into my coffee, sloshing it down the front of my clean tee-shirt. I laughed at that, too. This was going to be a great day.

With the sandwich stuck in my mouth, my refilled coffee mug in one hand and my duffle in the other, I pulled the Pink Door shut with my foot. Rover maintained a regal pose on the porch, his signal that he was content to man the fort while I was gone.

I took the long way to the highway, along the road next to the river and past some grazing land. There were daffodils blooming everywhere, and in one of the fields I noticed two new lambs. The sun was barely up and already these fluffy critters were cavorting like puppies. I pulled over to watch them play. They bounced and kicked, jousting with each other between the witless sheep whose heads never lifted from their grazing. The poor, dumb sheep had stopped having fun some seasons earlier.

"Lainey," I said out loud to myself, "never become a sheep."

The overall vibe in the caddie shack had changed with the weather. Maybe not everyone was in as good a mood as I was, but the happy definitely outnumbered the haunted.

"Top of the mornin' to you, Miss Lainey." Bushmills tapped the bill of his cap in greeting. "And how are you this fine day?"

"I am terrific. How 'bout yourself?"

"Couldn't be better. It looks to be a great day for golf, and I think even the likes of us will be out there for a loop or two."

"I've got my fingers crossed," I told him.

The door opened and I was surprised to see Rocks come in, trusty sidekick Corky at his heels. I unconsciously glanced at the wall clock and Rocks caught me.

"Yes, I'm here a little earlier than usual, Tidwell," he said with an exaggerated eye-roll. "Don't get excited."

I think I started to blush, but was saved by Bushmills.

"Whoa," he said. "What's going on here? Has the globe been jiggled off its axis? Or did you guys miss the switch to Daylight Savings Time two weeks ago and are just now catching up?"

"Don't start with that time-change thing, Bushmills. It makes me crazy," Rocks said.

"Yeah. I still don't get it," Corky chimed in.

Before Bushmills could deliver a punch line to that tee-up, Larson came in from his office looking more pressured than usual. He spoke into his two-way, looked at his clipboard, and then at us.

"What the hell. I'm desperate," he said, shrugging. "I need four caddies right now at the Hollows."

Bushmills pointed at himself, then me, then Rocks, then Corky, and said, "Three and a half. That should be close enough, sir."

"Hey!" Corky said, as the rest of us hurried to collect our gear.

"Shut up, dipwad," Rocks said. "How do you know he meant you?"

"Oh, yeah."

And we were off.

"SO, SANCHO PANZA, my dragon-fighting compatriot, I hear you had it pretty good today." Travis grinned at me before I even got close enough to give him a hug. "A foursome with four caddies – that's impressive. Not your basic cheapskate duffers then."

He stood at the bar next to Bushmills. I noticed an empty shot glass on the bar in front of Bushmills, who was halfway through a bottle of Budweiser. Travis looked like he'd just started his pint, and he signaled Jessica to get one for me.

"Jeez, Bushmills," I said. "How'd you get here so fast?"

"Well, what took *you* so long?" he replied. "I was motivated. A caddie develops a powerful thirst hand-holding a prima donna out in the tulles all day. At least your hack was playing golf. I don't know what mine was playing, but it was an interesting game. There were times I had to get the compass out to find our way back. We were in parts of the course I didn't know existed."

"And I missed you," I told him. "Corky and Rocks aren't so much fun."

"You and Rocks are still friends, huh?" Travis asked.

"I wouldn't say friends, but he hasn't called me Tit-swell lately."

Bushmills cringed. "Ah, good ol' Rocksy the Rake. I do believe the boy is improving. Corky, on the other hand…ay-ay-ay."

"Anyway, yes, Trav," I said, "I did have it pretty good today."

He kissed my forehead. Bushmills held up his bottle for a toast.

"Here's to a fine day of looping, and many more to come," he said, and the three of us clinked glasses.

Jessica came and stood across the bar from us, leaning in slyly.

"Lain, you gotta hear this. See those four women at the table?" She tilted her head towards a table by the jukebox. Seated there were four women who I could only describe as hardy. They were about the right age to be LPGA Seniors, and they certainly dressed the part. I spied logos on their shirts and visors from four well-known golf clubs, none of them Singing Bluffs.

"Yeah, we see them. Who are they?" I asked.

"I dunno. I don't think they're anybody. But who they're not, are big fans of Screaming Bluffs. They're on their third round of drinks and they've done nothing but bitch about your resort since they sat down."

"It's not *my* resort."

Bushmills asked, "Oh, yeah? Like what are they saying?"

"They're saying how they got treated like second-class citizens out there," Jessica said. "They are not happy campers."

"Oh, wow," Bushmills said. "We should talk to them, Lainey."

"I'm not talking to 'em. What would you want me to say? 'Hi, ladies. How was your round? Not so great, huh. Tell me about it – I work there.'"

He said, "Well, yeah. What's the matter with that?" He stood and took two dollar bills from his change on the bar. "Come on, Lainey. Help me pick some music."

I looked to Travis for help, but he said, "Oh, you go ahead. I'll hold your coat."

Jessica added, "Watch out for the one in the green hat. She's getting a little punchy."

143

At the jukebox, Bushmills was making a feeble attempt to look nonchalant. His eyes were on me, not the playlists, and he had his head tilted in their direction. Not that we had to strain to hear them...the ladies' voices carried easily and they obviously didn't care who heard them.

"Next year," one voice said, "we should have our reunion at Chambers Bay. That's a nice club up there."

"Sounds good to me. We can take pictures of us enjoying ourselves and post them on the Singing Bluffs Facebook page. Caption – Sorry, Bluffs. We're spending our money where you don't have to have a penis to golf."

Bushmills swung his head around so fast he almost fell over. I gripped his arm and turned him back to the jukebox.

"What galls me," the voice continued, "is that it wasn't just one or two assholes, it was how they permeated the stinking place."

Bushmills looked at me and mouthed, "Green hat."

"From the moment we parked the car, every man who walked by us seemed to make a point of staring at us like we had toilet paper hanging out of our pants."

"I thought the greeter at the pro shop was going to be okay, until we got upstaged by those jerks who jumped in front of us."

"We may as well have been bag ladies lookin' for a handout, the way the pro brushed us aside."

"I wish we'd told our caddies to go take a flying leap. The first time they snubbed us, we should've taken our bags from them and sent those boys packing. For all the good they were, we didn't need 'em. They sure didn't earn their fee, from my estimation."

"No shit. We were treated better by the volunteer at the turn stand. I gave that man a tip, but no way in hell was I going to tip the caddie."

"Well, it was some satisfaction to turn in our comments on the rating cards."

"Ha! You really think that's gonna do any good? They'll have a good laugh over it, that's all."

I left Bushmills at the jukebox and returned to sit next to Travis...my really great day shot to smithereens.

Chapter 23

TINY SUE SENT me a text message just as I was getting out of my Jeep. I could see her car across the nearly full parking lot, which meant I was late. Her texting me could mean I'd better hustle because she saw there was a good chance I could get a loop. Or it could mean I was in big trouble and she wanted to warn me. I decided to think positive and I hustled as I read her message.

"Just found out GM is back. Made appointment for 4. B will go with. Later. Gotta go."

Not the news I was hoping for.

As I crossed the lot, a shuttle bus pulled in and I saw Tiny Sue and Lyle running out of the shack. We crossed paths and I told her I'd just got her message.

"Yeah, Lain. Things are happening," Tiny Sue yelled back at me as she stepped into the bus. "I'll try to talk to you later. Bushmills told me about the ladies foursome at Pappy's yesterday. Can't wait to share that bit of PR. I tell you, girl, we're gonna blow this thing wide open."

"Oh, swell," I said, but they were already onboard and the driver shut the door.

I tried not to think as I went about the business of checking in and finding a place to sit. There were more caddies than the day before, and more who I didn't recognize. All of my senior caddie friends were missing, which meant they'd gotten assignments for early tee times.

At a table by the snack bar, I saw an empty chair and three first-years I knew so I went over to sit with them.

Long Johns said, "Hey, look who's here. Come join the party."

I thanked him and said hi to Cheech and Blinky.

Blinky, in his dry monotone, said, "She has to sit with us. There are no other seats available."

I started looking around to see if he was right, then realized that made me look desperate.

"For your information, Blinky, I don't *have* to sit with you – I want to. How's it been going with you guys anyway?"

Cheech said, "You know, some good days, lots of bad ones. We were just saying how that last storm just about did us in. Don't usually think about going south in March, but maybe I shoulda."

Long Johns said, "I think all these guys who came in today didn't come in yesterday because they didn't trust the sunshine. They waited twenty-four hours to make sure it took."

"Word is that tee times are comin' in more today than yesterday, too," Cheech said. "Maybe business is picking up."

They all nodded in agreement then went silent. These guys weren't the best conversationalists, but I thought it would be kinda rude to start reading my paperback in front of them, so time crawled. Finally, after two mind-numbing hours, Larson approached us.

"Davis, you've trained as a double-bagger, haven't you?" he asked Long Johns.

"Yes, sir," he answered.

I had a hard time picturing this scrawny kid weighed down by eighty pounds of clubs for over seven miles. I hoped he knew what he was getting into.

Larson went on, "Cheech, I know you're up for it. Both of you head out to the Bluffs. Lainey, Blinky, I'll send you two out with the next single-bag requests."

I didn't think it could get worse, but left on our own Blinky and I had absolutely nothing to talk about. When an easy chair opened up, I told him to go for it because he was here before I was.

"I don't want it. It's too far away from the TV. I'm watching this," he said.

I hadn't noticed. When I turned to see that "Who Wants to be a Millionaire" was on, I left him to it. The previously-owned paperback I'd just found at the Laundromat was calling me.

The book was one of John Sandford's Prey series with Lucas Davenport that I hadn't read. It had enough gory murders to keep me riveted until almost noon when Larson yelled for me and Blinky.

"We've got a twosome who called in late," Larson told us. "The Dusenberrys. Sounds like an older couple – their first time here and they want two caddies. I can fit them in right now, but there'll be a foursome teeing off at 12:30 so keep 'em moving."

"Will do," I said. Blinky was a little slower on the uptake, but we got outside before the shuttle arrived.

We were looping the Bluffs, same one Tiny Sue went to four hours earlier. I'd probably see her coming off the 18 as we left the first tee. Then I'd start stressing about the big meeting again. I gave myself a mental dope-slap and told myself to concentrate on giving this Dusenberry couple their best round of golf ever. I told Blinky that I would take the woman. Maybe it would give me some sense of balance for the lousy treatment given to the four women from yesterday.

We saw the couple as we approached the Bluffs curtain, and Tristan was doing a bang-up job of welcoming. He might have been overdoing it a bit, though, judging from the sound of things. I was upwind from them, farther than I could throw, and I heard him talking as if they were hard of hearing. They looked to be in their fifties and would have an easier time of walking eighteen holes than Tristan would. He was pushing nineteen and thought everyone older than Jimmy Fallon was ancient.

"Nice to meet you both," I said with the handshakes. Blinky mumbled something similar, and we picked up their respective bags.

As we walked to the tee box, Mrs. Dusenberry let out a gasp. "Oh! You're Lainey Tidwell. I just got the connection. Your picture was in *Northwest Golfer*, and you were quoted. You're the one, right?"

"Uh, yes, ma'am." I kept my head down so she couldn't see me cringe.

"Well, isn't this something!" she said. "Roy, remember her from that article? And now here I am with the famous Lainey Tidwell as my caddie."

I had to look up just to see if she was for real. Roy was too engrossed in his practice swings to reply, and Blinky, oblivious, was adjusting the bag straps on his shoulders.

"I'm not famous," I said when I realized she wasn't being sarcastic. "Hardly anyone here reads that magazine."

"Well, I find that hard to believe," she said. "I think it was a very interesting story. You sure opened my eyes to the world of caddying. The other women I golf with said as much, too. It really got us talking. Wait till I tell them I got you as my caddie. Boy, this is going to be fun!"

"Well, thanks for saying so. I'll try not to disappoint you."

"Oh, no way can you disappoint me, Lainey. I'm Doris, by the way," she said with a friendly smile. More seriously, she said, "Now, I want your advice about clubs. I know some golfers don't want that, but I need all the help I can get. I think I've got a pretty good swing, for a woman my age, but I've only played nice, neat and tidy, parkland courses. This will be a whole new experience."

"It will be a great experience, and I'll help you all you want."

Roy teed off, his ball making a pretty good line but too high. I hoped Blinky would give him some pointers about keeping it under the wind or it would kill him when we got near the bluff. Doris and I moved together to the red tees.

I used the same tone and words of advice that I used for golfers who, at the outset, showed they had respect for the game and for the course.

"I expect you've heard about the hard ground here, and I'm sure you'll get the hang of it after a couple of balls. Also, the wind will take another club or three more than you might be used to. I'll help remind you of that if you'd like."

"Oh, I'd like. And let me know if you see anything in my swing that I need to adjust. I'm really good at taking instructions," Doris said with a laugh. "I should. I've had plenty of them."

She teed up and took a powerful swing that sent the ball in a line drive that flew, then bounced, past Roy's ball on the fairway.

Doris handed me her club. "Well, what do you think?"

"Well, Doris, I think we're going to have some fun."

Chapter 24

DORIS AND ROY did it. Maybe Blinky even played a part in it. After the exchange of thank-yous and payment of fees, I rode back to the shack feeling invigorated. I had satisfaction for a job well done and a sense that all was right in my world again.

Both Blinky and I had been given only modest tips, but we weren't complaining. It was obvious, even to Blinky, that these people weren't the kind who had money to throw around. Their appreciation was expressed with looks of utter bliss – a bigger payoff to me than a few extra bucks from pompous, high-rolling snobs.

Not that we hadn't worked hard. Lost balls, added strokes, and poor understanding of the tight greens kept us on the go for all eighteen holes. But it was so fun. Doris couldn't contain herself whenever she looked around at the vast views beyond the bluffs. The sky put on a great show for us, with piles of white and grey fluffs circulating nonstop. The ocean was at its bluest and the snow-white surf was so gentle it rolled in slow motion. Doris took a ton of pictures.

"It's always like this," I told the Dusenberrys, but they knew I was joking. We joked the whole time. I love golfers who laugh at their own bad shots and sometimes forget what their score is.

Before I got off the shuttle my mind was made up. I wasn't even going to look for Tiny Sue. It was after four anyway, so if there really was a meeting with the general manager, it was either still going on or Sue and Bushmills were quickly dispatched and I didn't want to know why.

The beach was calling. I just needed a quick stop at the Pink Door for beach clothes and a shaggy friend who wouldn't mind a romp in the sand.

That made me think of Travis, so I called him as I drove out of the lot.

"Hey, Boom Boom. What's going on?" he answered.

"Hi. Who's Boom Boom?"

"Boom Boom. You know, Boomer. X-Force? Marvel Comics?"

"Nope. You're hitting nuthin' but hazards," I said.

"Never mind. I'm glad you called. Where are you?"

"On my way home, then to the jetty. Wanna join me?"

"Hell, yeah. Excellent idea. I'll finish up what I'm doing – I'm still at the site – and meet you there, okay?"

"Roger. Wilco. Boom Boom out," I said. Two can play at this game.

IT WAS DESERTED. It never fails to surprise me that this wonderful source of free entertainment is so close and so unappreciated. Maybe yesterday, the first day of sunshine after a long rain, was the day locals got their cabin fever cured. It was early season, though, and the valley folks would be flocking to the beach soon enough, so I had to enjoy the solitude while I could.

I kept Rover happy rummaging around the driftwood while we waited for Travis. It wasn't long before we heard his truck bumping through the potholes in the lot. I watched that broad-shouldered, self-assured yet laidback figure walking towards me and I turned into a lusting pile of mush. I guess my mind was in that euphoric state where everything was a turn-on.

We latched onto each other and made-out until we fell on our butts laughing in the sand.

"Wow. That was nice," Travis said when we'd caught our breath. "I don't know what's got into you, but I'm so, so glad you're sharing it with me."

"No one but you, Travis. If I've forgotten to mention it, I love you with every part of my being."

While we kissed some more, Travis murmured, "God, how I love every part of your being." Which struck us as funny and that broke up the make-out session just in time. We were starting to sink into the wet sand.

The sun was starting to get close to the horizon and there was a bank of long, layered clouds that promised a spectacular sunset. So after a short walk down the beach, we found a comfortable log to sit on and watch.

"Do you remember our first walk here?" Travis asked. "I was coming from the south, and I met up with you right about here."

"Do you think that was fate? That two people who hardly knew each other somehow ended up running into each other on a secluded beach, felt a connection, and then fell in love?"

"I dunno. It is a small town."

It didn't take me two seconds to deliver the punch in the arm he was really asking for.

"Ow. I'm sorry, sweetie. But who knows about fate? I mean really. Sometimes we have to take fate into our own hands. You know?"

"Yeah, I know," I said, snuggling into his chest again. I hated to think about it, though. I hated to think about anything except how great life was at that very moment.

"So I've been thinking," he said.

"*Really*? Now? Right now you want to tell me you've been thinking. Did you miss the part in romantic movies where the guy and the girl get all lovey-dovey watching the sun go down?"

"Uh, yeah. I guess so. I was more partial to the sun*rises* myself. But besides that, can I tell you what I've been thinking about?"

"Well, okay. Now that you've ruined it for me anyway, you might as well."

He was silent for a while, both of us facing the horizon – not each other.

"No, on second thought, I don't think I will."

I had my fist cocked and ready to deliver another punch but he was ready for it.

Laughing, he said, "I know, I know. That was a dirty trick. I didn't mean it. It's just that my mind is still processing an idea, and I don't want to pitch it to you until I've got all the bugs worked out."

"What am I, an investor?"

"Well, sort of," he said. "You won't have to wait very long. I promise. Right now I'm still in the inception stage, and that's kind of a one-man or -woman thing."

"What's the next stage, Mr. Madoff?"

"Getting buy-in from the partner. That's you."

At which point he kissed me, passionately, and I almost missed the sunset.

Chapter 25

TINY SUE CALLED as Travis and I were making dinner. He always had his fridge stocked with fresh vegetables, and his aunt and uncle kept him supplied with beef, so dinner at Travis's cabin was the easy choice. We were working together, slicing leftover grilled steak and veggies for a super salad when I heard "What Does the Fox Say?" coming from my pocket.

"Darth is singing," Travis said.

"I know."

"It's probably Tiny Sue. Aren't you going to answer it?"

"I'm still debating."

"Why? What's the worst that can happen?"

"She can tell me that she and Bushmills got the boot, with instructions to take their squirrely friend with them."

Travis wiped his hands on a towel and reached into my jeans pocket. Handing me the phone, he said, "Here. Get it over with."

He carefully took the knife out of my hand, and I bowed to Darth's bidding.

"Hello?"

"Lainey, glad I reached you," Tiny Sue said. "I didn't want to have to leave a message. This is too important."

"Really? What's goin' on?"

"Smitty listened to us, Lainey. He took it all in."

"That's nice. Who's Smitty?"

"Paul Smith, the GM. He told Bushmills and me to call him Smitty like everyone else does. He really seems like an okay dude. The bottom line is," Tiny Sue said, pausing to take a breath, "you can stop worrying. That article with your name in it, and all that it exposed, won't hurt you. In fact, it has made you a rock star, baby."

"Oh shit."

I had to sit down. Travis guided me into a chair and set a fresh beer down in front of me.

Tiny Sue was still talking. "There's lots more to tell you, but I'm exhausted and it can wait. I just wanted to give you the lowdown before I turned my phone off. I knew you'd be waiting to hear how the meeting went."

"Yeah...uh...thanks," was all that I could get out.

"Lain, you okay?" she asked.

"Yeah, I think so. Thanks for calling. Really."

"Where are you, girl? I'm just asking so I know you're really okay."

"I'm at Travis's."

"Okay. That's good. Tell him hi for me. And relax, kid. Everything is going to work out."

I repeated what she'd said to Travis and the combination of his cool reaction and hearing the words from my own mouth relaxed me.

"You know, I've heard that about Smitty," Travis said. "That he's a fair guy to work with. He's got a head for the golf business, that's for sure, and he doesn't seem to be afraid to take risks, to be the first to step ahead of the pack."

He put plates on the table and began making salad dressing. I showed some initiative and got up to get the silverware and napkins.

While he worked, Travis kept talking in his easy-going, upbeat tone. "Like, taking that piece of scrub land and envisioning a golf resort in the first place was a huge leap of faith. And he did his homework, working with the agencies, showing respect for the environment, hiring the right people and giving them the same vision. I can appreciate all of that, now that we're going through the same process at Azalea Leas."

He put the cruet on the table and I retrieved the salad bowl from the fridge. Something about the smooth pace and balance that passed between us as we worked together felt sexy. I was just beginning to imagine the two of us in a slow, romantic dance, when Travis turned on his music system. He found some Green Day, turned the volume low, and we sat down to eat.

Between mouthfuls, I said, "Yum...this is almost too delicious to be healthy."

"Better than Cheez-Its and deli coleslaw?"

"Uh-huh. Much. Not that I'm willing to give up Cheez-Its and coleslaw completely, but I might just cut back a bit."

I looked across the table at him, his eyes shining through the lenses of his glasses and sending me a message so strong that it felt like it could last a lifetime.

"Sweetheart, I would never ask you to give up Cheez-Its. Trust me," he said with mock seriousness. "I'm not that brave."

"What about deli coleslaw?"

"Ah. Now that, I think, I might persuade you to step up a notch. Aunt Gail has a great recipe, as a matter of fact, and she grows her own cabbage."

"Yeah, I know. I love it. But I can't expect her to be at my beck and call whenever I need to round out my empty-carbs-and-beer diet with something green. And it's not like I have the wherewithal to shred cabbage and carrots and whatnot."

"Wanna know what that 'whatnot' is?" he asked, forking a radish slice and pointing it in my direction.

"No."

"Have you ever looked at the ingredients of Ranch Dressing?"

"No."

"Would it surprise you to know that it can be made fresh with buttermilk and a few herbs?" he said with an evil grin.

"No," I replied, but immediately betrayed myself by adding, "Eew."

We continued bantering and eating until nothing was left but a few bits of gristle, which Rover had dibs on. As we cleared the table, a mellow love song began playing and we started moving with the music, getting closer. I took the last dirty plate from his hands and put it in the sink. Then I took him by the hand and led him the two steps into the middle of the cabin.

For the kind of dancing we were in the mood for we didn't need much room.

THERE'S NOTHING LIKE a good night's sleep, and every night at the cabin with Travis meant a good night's sleep. His homemade bed was so comfortable. I had a theory that it was because it was a good foot higher than mine, so it gave me the sensation of floating on air. Travis says that's nuts. With your eyes closed, you can't tell the difference. Whatever. I will continue to dream of flying.

Then there were the sounds. At the Pink Door, the noise from the highway was a constant detraction. At the cabin, I heard the wind in the trees, frogs croaking, night critters skittering in the brush, birds singing and Aunt Gail's rooster crowing in the mornings. Travis didn't ever use an alarm to wake up. Whenever I stayed there, we both woke up before full daylight with enough time for a quick snuggle, then hit the ground running.

This morning was no different. Again, our movements reminded me of an old married couple, only with the energy of the hip-and-happening.

"So, what's your schedule like today?" I asked.

"I've got about two hours of work left to do on the latest terrain model, then Andy and I have a phone meeting with the irrigation contractor."

"Wow. It's getting exciting, huh?"

"I'm having the time of my life, Lainey," he said, getting the steamy look he gets when his mind is really cooking.

"Hey, you called me Lainey. What's up with that? Don't I rate a stupid nickname this morning?"

He handed me my travel mug of coffee, gave me a quick kiss, and said, "You have an exciting day yourself, Katniss."

I glared at him. "I bet you think I don't know who that is, don't you?"

"That's right, I don't think you do. So I'll give you a hint. Katniss *can* kick ass."

"I knew that."

He just smiled as he put on his coat, grabbed his coffee mug, and went out the door into the early morning chill. For five seconds I considered phoning Jessica and waking her up to ask her who the hell was Katniss.

Chapter 26

DAMNED IF ROCKS didn't surprise me again. He was even nice about it and didn't make fun of me for not knowing about Katniss.

"Guess you haven't seen *The Hunger Games* movie," he said. "Katniss Everdeen is the heroine. Jennifer Lawrence plays her."

"I've heard of the books," I said, establishing that I wasn't totally out of touch. Although why I felt like I had to prove myself to Rocks I didn't know. "It's a trilogy, isn't it?"

"I dunno," he said with a shrug. "I've only seen the one movie so far. It's pretty good. You should stream it on your computer, or iPad or whatever."

"Yeah, okay. I'll try to remember to do that. Thanks for the tip."

This new camaraderie with Rocks wasn't chummy enough for me to reveal the fact that I didn't have a computer or an iPad or whatever. It might be possible to "stream" a movie on my smartphone, but if it were I wasn't aware of it. Maybe someday I'll get adventurous enough to take that up with Darth.

It was a quiet morning in the caddie shack, which is why Rocks overheard me asking Tucson Johnny if he knew who Katniss was. Then Johnny got called up for a loop and I was left standing with Rocks, Corky, and some guy I didn't know. It got awkward when their conversation turned to their favorite movies with hot babes in them, and I looked for somewhere else to go.

Then Bushmills came in from the back smoking area and grinned when he saw me.

"Hey, whadda ya say, kiddo?"

"Not much, Bushmills. I'm surprised you're here. Do you have a late-morning assignment?" I asked.

"No, I don't," he said matter-of-factly. "You see, the Artful Dodger is still in charge, so I don't expect I'll get any work as long as that is the case."

I felt bad for him, but I couldn't resist asking the obvious question. "Then why do you stick around? If you know he's not going to give you a loop, why are you here instead of heading to another club?"

"Oh, well, I had to come to see what happens." He glanced around the caddie shack eagerly.

"What happens? What do you mean by that?"

Instead of answering, he looked over my shoulder and his eyes lit up.

"Well, speak of the devil," he said.

I turned to see Art coming in from Larson's office. Technically, it was Art's office, since he was the chief supervisor of caddie services, Larson's boss. But Art didn't spend much time there. Rumor had it that he did most of his business in the VIP bar of the lodge and could be seen schmoozing in the pro shops on occasion. Not only was it odd to see him walk into the caddie shack, it was one of the rare times that he didn't have a phone stuck to his ear.

Just as he was about to pass by the front door, Tiny Sue opened it and walked in, nearly running into him. She politely pulled the door back and stepped out of his way.

"Oh, sorry about that, Art," was all she said. But the way she said it made me think she wasn't sorry at all.

Art didn't reply. He just scrunched up his bulldog face and glared at Tiny Sue as if she'd spit on him. He walked on without saying anything, then bumped his way through the room turning his head like he was searching for someone. I say bumped, because he kept running into chairs, caddies, garbage cans – it was like he had blurred vision and had to make it through a maze. Whenever he hit something, he just bounced off and re-aimed himself towards the locker room.

Bushmills joked, "Looks like old Mr. Magoo there isn't having a very good day."

Tiny Sue added, "Like maybe he got some bad news and isn't thinking too clearly. Ya gotta wonder why he decided to make an appearance in the shack this morning."

"Yeah, you'd think he'd want to stay clear the hell away from caddies today...except for his fan club, that is." Bushmills scanned the room for a moment, then said, "Where are they all? I don't see one of the Artful Dodger's troop of irregulars."

"Maybe that's what he was looking for," I said. "Didn't it look like he was looking for something, or someone?"

"If I didn't know any better," Tiny Sue said, "I'd think some rats have already left their sinking ship."

Bushmills gave her a startled look. "They couldn't know anything. Not that fast. Unless...you don't think Smitty gave 'em their pink slips, do you?"

"Nah, I wouldn't think so. Not yet, anyway," Tiny Sue said. "Probably just a coincidence."

"What are you guys talking about?" I asked, my voice starting to rise. "You're both talking crazy."

Tiny Sue tilted her head towards a vacant sitting area in the back of the room. "Come on, let's sit down. I'll tell you about the meeting yesterday."

None of the other caddies paid any attention as the three of us drifted to the back corner.

"Well, it was like I said on the phone last night," Tiny Sue began as we sat. "Smitty greeted us, all friendly like, told us to call him Smitty, and said he was curious what we wanted to see him about."

Bushmills started to say something, but she held up her hand to hold him off.

"I said that I'd been concerned about some of the caddie service policies for a while and things had finally come to a head. Then he asked Bushmills if he had the same concerns..."

"And I said, 'Yes, sir, I sure do,' and then he sat there and listened to every one of our complaints."

"What, did you have a list or something?" I asked, imagining a scene from *Erin Brockovich*.

Tiny Sue said, "We had a few notes. Didn't want to forget anything."

"Like, what kind of things?" I asked.

"We began with how assignments were being based on an unfair system of favoritism, not seniority and competency as stated in the caddie handbook."

Bushmills cut in again. "I took a copy in with us and pointed out the parts that were downright fabrications and those that were ambiguous."

"Yeah," Tiny Sue said, "that really helped. He agreed that there were some parts that needed changing. Then I brought up how you'd been worried about retaliation for talking to that journalist. He said that wouldn't happen, that he thought the article was interesting and had opened his eyes to some things. He'd already started to have concerns about the image of the resort, like maybe it wasn't as respectable as he'd hoped."

"We told him that the so-called 'Code of Conduct' was a joke," Bushmills said. "Everybody knows what it says in the handbook, but in reality it's perfectly fine to trash-talk women and any person of non-white heritage. In other words, anyone who doesn't look like Miami. I said that if he really wanted us to be stewards of the game, like we want to be, he'd put some teeth in that 'Code.' And we weren't just talking about the caddies. I told him about the lady golfers who'd been dissed and were talking it up in the tavern. He was horrified. Wasn't he?"

He looked at Tiny Sue, who nodded emphatically.

"He really was. Then, Lainey," she said, drawing in closer, "I dropped the bomb. I related the whole story of Art inviting me to the VIP clubhouse. Then I played the recording of him coming on to me and threatening to fire me if I didn't have sex with him."

"Oh, gawd. You really did?" I asked. My head was spinning with visions of them in Smith's office, exposing all these sleazy things straight to his face.

"You bet I did," she replied. "He got very still and his eyes bored right into me."

"I think he was grinding his teeth," Bushmills said.

Sue went on, "He asked if I knew of any other women who'd been harassed. I said I did. So did Bushmills."

"So does every caddie in here," he said. "We all know what the female caddies have to put up with. But everyone just lets it slide. It's gotten so that it's an accepted practice and girls use it to their advantage."

"Not all of us," I was quick to point out.

"Oh, I know that. And everyone here knows that's why Art holds you and Sue back. Larson does what he can to equalize things, but he's fighting a losing battle with the Artful Dodger holding the reins."

Tiny Sue stood up and began her usual down-time stretching routine.

"Hopefully that won't be for too much longer," she said as she flexed a biceps.

Bushmills watched her for a moment, then said, "Okay, now you're just showing off."

"Bite me, old-timer. If my exercise is exhausting you, maybe you should take a nap." She let out a long exhale. "We might as well make ourselves comfortable while we wait for Art's meltdown."

Chapter 27

IT WAS A STRANGE feeling being one of only three caddies in on a secret with the potential power to shock the whole squad. I felt like I knew the surprise ending to a soon-to-be-released suspense thriller they were dying to see. Bushmills, Tiny Sue, and I agreed to keep everything hush-hush in case it went bust and nothing happened. Art drew puzzled looks each time he came bumbling through the room, nervously looking around but not speaking to anyone. It was hard not to tell what I knew. I had the all-time spoiler and barely enough scruples to keep my mouth shut about it.

It was okay to tell Travis, they said, so I went outside to an empty picnic table and phoned him.

"So, did they get a good feeling that Smitty was going to do something?" Travis asked.

"Yeah, they're pretty positive about it. He told them he was aware of some problems with the roster and complaints about shack rules, but Art had assured him that it was just a few disgruntled upstarts. Smitty told Sue and

Bushmills that he didn't consider them disgruntled upstarts and he thanked them for coming in."

"Okay! It sounds good. So-o-o, have you started to feel more confident about committing to your chosen career yet? Or are you still thinking of throwing in the towel and putting your application in at Walmart?"

I detected the touch of a dopeslap in his tone.

"It could go either way, wiseass. I'm still on the fence." My attitude was getting fired up now. "Of course, I would feel a whole hell of a lot better if I had a freaking loop. Here it is ten o'clock on a gorgeous morning, a perfect day for golf, and three of Singing Bluffs' best caddies are sitting on their butts with a bunch of dopey bag-packers."

"That's my girl," he said. "You've got your groove on now!"

I laughed. "You're really not helping me. Don't you have work to do?"

"Yeah, I really should get back to it."

"What are you working on? Did you have your conference with the irrigation guy?"

"Oh, yeah. It went really well. We should start that phase next week, and that'll keep me busting ass for a while. Andy wants me working with the layout every step of the way, since that was one of my best fields when I trained in Silverton."

"Good. I'm glad one of us is working. Will you buy me a beer once in a while, if you have the time?"

"If I have the time. And, if you relax and quit panicking about losing your job."

"Okie-dokie. You got a deal. Now go to work, and I'll talk to you later."

"Okie-dokie. Good-bye, Lucy."

Ha! I had this one. "Good-bye, Ricky."

I got up off the table and kicked around the yard for a while, not yet willing to go back in to face the people I'd called dopey bag-packers. I noticed two guys were putting on the caddie practice green near the parking lot. They had been somewhat friendly a time or two, although I had never worked with them, so I went over to say hi.

"How's it goin'?" the older of the two said.

"Pretty good," I said. "How you guys doin'?"

"Can't putt worth a shit," he said as his ball missed a three-footer by half a roll.

He had dark skin and longish hair sticking out from under a Titleist cap. The younger one, a baby-faced kid with the caddie sunburn that showed where his sunglasses had been, said, "You lose again, Frisco. That's ten bucks."

The older one sneered at him. "Keep a tab, why don't ya? We've got all day."

Their smiles told me they didn't mind me hanging around, so I said, "Frisco, huh. Is that your nickname, like where you're from?"

"Nah, it's my real name. My parents were hippies." He lined up a twenty-footer on the green. "I'm from Hawaii."

I waited for him to take his shot, which he left way short, and said, "Wow. Hawaii. That's cool. What brought you to Oregon?"

"That's a good question," he said as he marked his ball, not bothering to answer.

"I'm Joe," said the baby face.

"Just plain Joe? No nickname?"

"Nope, just Joe." He putted the same shot as Frisco, leaving it on the lip.

"Nice shot," I said. He tapped it in, grinning at Frisco, and I kept talking. "I don't have a nickname, either. Not a real one, anyway." I hoped they hadn't heard the ones Rocks called me...before he became less of a creep than he used to be, anyway.

"We know who you are," Frisco said.

"Yikes. Should I be worried?"

"No, not at all," he said.

At that moment, Art came out of the back of the building and scurried across the parking lot towards the admin offices.

"Wonder what Art's got his boxers in a bunch about," Frisco said. "Is it just me, or is he acting squirrellier than usual today?"

Joe shook his head in disgust. "Pitiful. That ain't no way to run a golf course. This guy's gotta learn to chill, have some fun in life."

"Oh, I wouldn't worry about that, Joe. I'm pretty sure Art's been gettin' his share of fun."

They both snickered, making me uncomfortable.

I cleared my throat and made an attempt to mosey on.

Frisco stopped me by saying, "Hey, I liked the way you came off in that interview in *Northwest Golfer,* by the way."

"Uh-huh. I suppose you really liked the accompanying photo of me, too. Or did you like the one on the bulletin board better?"

They chuckled, and Joe said, "Yeah, that was pretty funny. Classic Miami."

"No, really," Frisco said, "it's a good article. That chick writer scored some decent points."

"Yeah, there's a whole lot goin' on around here that Smitty oughta be takin' a look at," Joe added. "Maybe now he will."

"I wouldn't hold my breath."

"Huh." That was all I could think of to say.

I waited to watch them go for another wager, to see if Frisco could find the bottom of the cup before Joe did. On a whim, I said to Frisco, "Try singing a song to yourself."

He said, "Whuh?"

"As you're setting up, start a song in your head. Pick something you like, and hum it or just sing it in your head, and keep it there as you stroke. I've heard it works."

He gave me a doubting look, then set his putter-head behind the ball. Several seconds passed, then he smoothly brought his club back. When the face came forward, it came in dead-square contact and the ball rolled off beautifully. It went the twenty feet directly to the cup and dropped.

Joe yelled, "No way! I don't believe it. What fuckin' song did you sing, Dude?"

Frisco smiled, "Not telling."

I grinned at them both then I walked back to the shack. The activity level of the slouches in front of the TV hadn't changed, but the number of loopers dinking around the snack bar area had grown. Bushmills was regaling some newbies with stories of his past, which I would've enjoyed,

173

but I saw that Tiny Sue was pacing by herself near the back wall.

I approached, leaving a wide track for her to continue the trajectory in progress, and asked, "Did I miss anything?"

"Only another one of Art's restless rambles through the room a minute ago. Still hasn't said a word to anyone. Doesn't even give a nod to the suck-ups who tried to say hi to him."

"Weird. Why'd he come here, anyway? He could've stayed in the lodge, or gone out on a course with some of his cronies like usual. It's creepy seeing him hang around for so long."

"I think he must've gotten a heads-up from someone that the GM might be comin' down on his ass. He's making a show of actually working with caddies, in the caddie shack, where you'd expect to find a caddie director. But he's so totally freaked out he's making a bigger fool of himself than he normally does."

"He headed up to the admin office when he left here," I told her.

"Good. Maybe he'll find a bottle in a desk up there and get himself good and hammered."

We stood silently for a couple of minutes, taking in the inescapable dreariness of our surroundings.

Tiny Sue suddenly snapped her fingers. "Hey, that's not a bad idea."

"What isn't?"

"Getting ourselves hammered. We're not accomplishing anything here, so we should just blow this dive and go to a better one."

"If you say so," I said. "You're the role model. I'll see you there."

Chapter 28

THREE MORE UNBEARABLE days went by with nothing but delusional fantasies and nervous perspiration circulating in the shack. It was worse than boredom. With boredom I could let my mind wander. But with the pendulum of doom hanging over our heads, I felt like I had to make my mind work to solve the puzzle. Which was impossible since I didn't have a clue what kind of puzzle it was, let alone have faith that my mind could solve it.

So Bushmills, Tiny Sue, and I wasted ourselves away for the better part of each day. We came early and stayed late, on the off chance that something, *anything*, would happen. If just one of us had gotten a loop, we would've cheered like the gallery on the 16th hole at TPC Scottsdale. I would've paid half a month's rent if it could get Larson to call Tiny Sue for a single bag on the last tee time of the day. But Larson came and went, calling every other loser in the shack at one time or another, and couldn't even look us in the eye.

On the afternoon of the third day, just before our self-imposed cutoff time of 2:00, Larson intercepted Tiny Sue as she came out of the bathroom. I just happened to look up at the right time as I was taking my tidying tour through the caddie shack. Because the complex had no housekeeping staff and we were obligated to clean up after ourselves, the task got done to varying degrees of success. Each caddie had a different definition of *clean*. I usually made an effort to do my part by disposing of my own water bottles and sandwich wrappers. But sometimes I didn't because, face it, when you're in the mental stupor that hours in a caddie shack can induce, chores can be neglected. So I made up for those messes left behind by occasionally cleaning up after the rest of the slobs and making a big show of it.

Which was why I almost missed seeing Larson stop Tiny Sue in the hallway and take her into his office. He wasn't smiling, but he wasn't frowning either. Not that that told me anything because Larson's face rarely gave away any emotion. I looked around to see if anyone else noticed their exit, and caught Cheech's eye. He gave me a quizzical look and shrugged before getting back to his card game. I went outside to find Bushmills where he always was this time of day, holding down his end of the picnic table in the smoking area.

"Hey, Ms. Tidwell, my good lass. What do you have to say for yourself this fine afternoon?"

"Easy for you to say," I told him. "I don't know that it's such a fine afternoon. I'm close to going stark raving mad if I have to spend another consecutive day sitting on my ass in there."

He gave me his happy grin, exhaled cigarette smoke, and shook his head slowly – his way of winding up to deliver an exclusive comment.

I stopped him before he could speak. "But that's not what I want to talk to you about. I just witnessed the weirdest thing."

"Oh, wow. That's really saying something, considering our cultural happenstance."

"I'm not kidding. Larson just came and got Tiny Sue and took her into his office."

His smile disappeared. Then he said, "Why? Is she in trouble for something, anything you know of?"

"No. I don't think so. She was sucker-punched, Bushmills. I'm sure she didn't even see it coming. What do you think is going on?"

"I don't have a clue, except that it's probably not good. Larson only asks to see us, privately like that, when we've been caught."

"But Sue hasn't done anything," I whined. "You both told me Art couldn't get any of us fired. You said the worst he could do is hold back loops, and he's already doing that. So what else could possibly go wrong?"

"I swear, Lainey. Mr. Smith assured us that we were within our rights to talk to him like we did, and that our jobs as caddies weren't in jeopardy. I think if he even knew we haven't gotten a loop since, he'd be madder than a slug on a saltlick."

He got up and started pacing. I sat down and started biting my nails. The pacing must have been more productive because after a minute he said, "You know what? I've gotta go see the GM. I'm just praying he hasn't taken off on another pleasure trip."

He stubbed out his smoke and started hotfooting it towards the lodge.

"Wait," I yelled. "Don't you want to wait until Tiny Sue comes out? Maybe there's nothing to worry about. I'm sure she'll be here in a minute and she can tell us what happened."

But I was wrong. I went back inside and saw that Larson was on the phone in his office, and there was no sign of Tiny Sue.

"Hey, did any of you see Tiny Sue leave?" I asked the table full of card players and lurkers.

Cheech spoke up. "You just missed her. She's gone for the day."

"What? Not again," I wailed. "Dammit! Well, did you see her come out of Larson's office?"

The only affirmation I got was Blinky nodding definitively without looking up from his hand, which, if they were playing poker, would've been good for lowball. From his perplexed expression, I gathered that wasn't the game.

"Well, how did she look?" I asked him.

"Who?" he said.

"Tiny Sue, you numbnuts! How did she look when she came out of the office?"

He hesitated, as if thinking hard, then said, "Short."

A round of sluggish snorts of what I assumed was laughter came from the crowd, and I gave up. I got my gear and went to my Jeep. Once there, however, I became inert.

All I could think about was that I wished I had brought my dog.

With no one to hug, I resorted to Darth. I punched in Tiny Sue's number.

"Yo! Who's this?" her chirpy voice answered.

"Sue! What the hell? How come you left without saying anything?"

"Oh, hi Lainey. Boy, that didn't take long. I'm only just at the highway."

"Well, what did you think? I saw you and Larson talking. What's going on?"

I heard a noise like air coming out of a tire, and realized it was Sue exhaling a slow leak into her Bluetooth.

"It's complicated," she finally said. "I don't want to…no, it's really that I can't…I can't say anything before you hear it from the powers that be."

"You can't be serious. It's *me*, Sue. What can't you tell *me*?"

"It's nothing bad, Lainey. Really. I'd tell you if it was bad. Please just trust me on that, and hang on another while longer. It's all good. Gotta hang up now, but I'll see you first thing tomorrow."

I was left with a void in my ear and still no one to hug.

As I was about to turn the ignition, I saw Bushmills making a beeline for his car.

"Wait up!" I called.

He perked up from the depths of whatever contemplation had hold of his brain and turned to meet me.

"Lainey, wow," he said, as we got close enough to talk in private tones. "You are not going to believe this. The weirdest thing..."

"No-o-o," I screamed. "Not...another...weird...thing. I can't take any more."

"Sorry, sorry. It's okay. It's not really that weird. It's sort of in the context of *special*, or I might even go so far as to say..."

"Stop! Bushmills, please don't *even* go that far. What the fuck is happening here?"

"I don't know," he said very seriously. "We have to wait to find out. I was just told that the General Manager himself is calling a meeting. A meeting that all caddies who are registered with Singing Bluffs Resort are required to attend."

Chapter 29

IT TOOK SEVERAL minutes of staring at my cellphone to muster the guts to press the all-too familiar logo and read the text.

Singing Bluffs Caddie Services 4:30PM Important! Mandatory meeting scheduled for tomorrow, 5:00pm, Madrone Hall, next to administration building. All caddies' attendance required to receive alerts of changes in current policies. Your absence may result in losing your place on the assignment roster.

After reading and re-reading the text message, I sat on the couch with Rover's head on my lap, feeling sorry for myself for another twenty minutes. That was how long it took before Travis returned my call and said he was really swamped and didn't have time to talk. He said, "Sorry, babe. I'll have to call you later," and disconnected.

"Well, screw this," I told Rover. "Let's go to Pappy's."

As soon as I said "Pappy's" it was like a switch was thrown in the little guy's head and he was hot to trot. Ears perked and tail wagging, Rover expressed exactly what he knew I wanted to hear. He knew we'd had enough mopey cuddling – it was time to get off our butts and go downtown. A good dog's empathetic power knows no bounds.

I walked into the tavern just as Jessica got off her shift. The bar was full but Twitch had saved a stool for her. When they saw me, they waved me over and Jess nudged the guy next to her with her elbow.

"Yo, dude," she said. "Can't you see there's a lady standing. She needs a beer, too."

The poor guy was startled into standing, and reached for his money as he called Curly over.

"That's all right," I told him. "You don't have to buy my beer, but I will take the seat. Thanks."

He gave me an embarrassed smile and gave Jess an uneasy glance.

"Seriously, Jess," I said, "you should stop harassing your customers, especially when they're strangers. He probably doesn't know how to take you."

"One, I'm now on this side of the bar so he's not my customer. Two, he's no stranger than any of the other bums in here. And three, he should've known I was joking when I called you a lady."

"Thanks a lot, pal," I said. "I came down here to get cheered up, not to get insulted."

Curly served me a frosty pint of perfectly drawn beer (filled to the rim with only a nickel's head of foam) and said, "See if this helps." He deftly scooped up my money and lumbered his Samurai bulk back to the cash register.

"See, Jess. That's how a good bartender treats his customers," I said. The stranger standing next to me gave a silent thumbs up.

"Right. I'll try to remember that. So, anyway, Lain, where's Travis? Did he slip his leash tonight?"

"Had to work late." I shrugged and sipped my beer, trying to show that I wasn't perturbed. "Where's Joe?"

Jess made a sad face and said, "He had to go north. That route always takes all day. Evidently there are a lot of jukeboxes at that end of the county. He'll end up staying at his house, too tired to drive down to see me."

We sighed simultaneously. I said, "I guess we know how we rate – way behind golf courses and juke joints."

Twitch, who had been involved in the conversation going on next to him, caught the tail end of ours. "Now you two shouldn't be grumbling like that. Your beaus have good jobs, like both of you have. That's something to be proud of. They're both very nice fellas and I know they think the world of you, so no more bellyaching."

As usual, Twitch said just the right thing to reach through my clouded brain and get a smile out of me.

"Sorry, Twitch. You're absolutely right. I am proud of Travis and glad he's doing something he enjoys."

"Yeah, well," Jess said, "I don't know that Joe is in love with tending jukeboxes, but it pays the bills. Hey, you know what? We're talking about moving in together."

Twitch and I swiveled on our stools to face her. She looked at each of us and said, "Well, don't look so surprised. We're in love, aren't we? And we're spending almost every night together anyway, so it would save gas and time. Think of what we'd save sharing one house instead of two."

"There's a lot more to living with someone than sharing expenses, Jessica," Twitch said. His somber expression gave me the feeling that he was thinking of his wife, whom I knew he still missed very much.

"Of course there is. Anyway, I just said we were thinking about it," Jess said.

I wasn't going to let her get off that easily. The fact that she was even considering living with her boyfriend, without ever once discussing that eventuality with me, was unexpected. Jess and I were smart, free-thinking, modern women. We had no ties. As my father put it, we were in-de-*goddam*-pendent. It was crazy to think we'd ever want to give up that kind of freedom.

"Twitch is right, Jess. Living with someone is a huge deal. Whose house would it be, yours or his? Either way, one of you is still going to be driving the same amount that you do now. If you move in with him you'd have to drive here to work everyday. Or would you quit Pappy's? Have Joe support you. Is that the plan?"

"Gawd, I don't know. Why are you hassling me? I don't have a plan. I'm just thinking."

We all sipped beers without speaking for a moment. Then I said, "Well, if you do quit, I think I'll apply for your position."

Twitch chuckled and Jessica erupted with a loud, "Ha!"

"Why not?" I said. "I could tend bar."

"No you couldn't. You're way too sensitive. You think the caddie shack is gross – eight hours of this place and you'd be needing either your mommy or a good shrink."

Before I could think of a comeback, Twitch said, "I think maybe we should change the subject." He tilted his head a smidge, indicating the guys still talking on the other side of him. "The boys here tell me there is some kind of mysterious meeting at the Bluffs tomorrow, Lainey. What do you suppose that's all about?"

I huffed a breath so hard up my face that my bangs flew. "All I know is that I got a text message about an hour ago saying all caddies had to be there tomorrow at five. Something about a change in policies."

"Uh-huh. That's what they heard."

"There's more," I told him. "Tiny Sue and Larson had a weird confab behind closed doors today, and she can't tell me what it was about. But she assured me it wasn't anything bad."

Jess snorted. "Oh, that's comforting. Maybe he was asking her for fashion advice because he's designing new jumpsuits for you loopers."

Twitch chuckled again and began the slow rise to his feet. I noticed he'd somehow emptied his glass when we weren't looking, his trick to dodge any offer to have another.

"Well, you keep us posted. We all like to hear about what's going on at Singing Bluffs. I'll be off now. See you lovely ladies soon."

He shuffled towards the door and Jess said, "You know that thing he said about everyone wanting to know what's happening at Screaming Bluffs?"

"Yeah?"

"He was joking."

Chapter 30

I DROVE THROUGH the caddie parking lot three times looking for Tiny Sue's car. It was late enough in the morning that she should have already checked in. I thought I had the timing right for catching her before she got a bag – *if* she got a bag. But I didn't know what to think of the fact that she hadn't come to work. She had told me she'd see me first thing. So where the hell was she?

Even with Travis's late-night pillow talk, I still felt my world was out of whack. Of course, it would've helped had he expressed his sympathies while lying in bed next to me and not by phone, but he did try. As tired as he sounded, I shouldn't have expected him to do anything besides go straight to his cabin after a long day's work. I really am mature enough to know it isn't always about me. But sometimes being a smart, free-thinking, independent woman can be a bitch.

I braced myself for the impact of a caddie shack in full frenzy mode and went inside. There were different huddles of gab sessions stationed around the room, the televisions were turned off, and no one was sleeping on the couches. I searched for a friendly face and saw Jake raising both eyebrows at me. I took that to be an invitation and went to sit with him.

"Good morning," I said, trying to sound cheerful, as if the all-points bulletin like the one we'd all received went out on a regular basis.

"Hey, Lainey. Don't ask me what's going on because I don't have any idea."

"Okay, I won't. And I don't have any idea either, so we're even. You going out today?"

"On the Bluffs in a few minutes. You?"

"Not that I know of, but I'm here anyway, sitting at attention like a good little newbie."

He smiled and nodded in understanding. There was so much chatter going on around us that I guessed that neither of us felt like talking. From pieces of conversations that rose above the din here and there, I gathered that there was only one topic. Some old-timers boasted knowingly that there wasn't anything to worry about, that the meeting was just to tell us our annual fee was going up or that all caddies would be expected to double-bag from now on. Others claimed the urgency of the message meant only one thing – the dreaded, delayed high season and inevitable cut backs in the squad.

I saw Bushmills leave one of the groups and head our way. He had a nimble spring in his step that matched the impish gleam in his eye. The sight made Jake chuckle. It made me worry.

"Well, this is fun, isn't it?" he said with a little hunch of his shoulders. "It's not every day we have this much to keep us amused."

"Glad to see you're enjoying yourself," Jake said. "You're not concerned about why we're being summoned to this policy meeting that came out of the blue?"

"Nope," he answered.

"Nothing ever bothers you, does it?"

"I sure can't think of anything. It's a beautiful day, there's the possibility of being a part of some good golf, and there's still no sign of the Artful Dodger skulking about. Life is good."

"Sheesh," I said. "I wish I had your optimistic outlook. I'm developing ulcers and you'll probably live to be a hundred."

"Well, sure. Why not?" His sunburned face held a grin and his eyes flashed.

Jake and I stood in silence, taking in the wonder that was Bushmills.

Then Jake glanced at the clock and said, "I gotta go catch the bus. You kids hang in there, and I guess I'll see you later at the meeting."

"Yep," Bushmills said. "You sure will."

I didn't particularly want to listen to the caddies' speculations any more, but Bushmills did so we parted company and I sat down to read. On my way to a good chair, I passed the magazine rack and noticed the current copy of *Northwest Golfer*. I *so* wanted to read Pat's article again to remind myself of what all the hubbub was about, but I couldn't risk letting someone see me. Undoubtedly, there would be a picture of me reading it on the bulletin the next day, complete with nasty embellishments.

So I passed the magazines and got out my paperback. I had read only a couple of pages when I heard Larson come in from his office. He called Bushmills and, to my great amazement, me. We were going to loop Hemlock Hollows.

"Bushmills, you've got a pair, and Tidwell, looks like you're assigned to...uh," he hesitated, checking his clipboard, "one Tiger Woods."

"Wow, Lainey," Bushmills said into the silence that followed. "This must be your lucky day."

I knew he meant that sarcastically because he didn't think much of the celebrated Masters champion.

"I don't think so, Mr. Larson. Nice try, but I'm not buying it."

"Okay, it may not be *the* Tiger Woods. 'Tiger' is in quotation marks here. Regardless, get out there."

SINCE TRAVIS WON a year's worth of greens fees for his ace at last season's fundraising tournament, we'd been on the course together only once, when I'd caddied on the Bluffs for one of his playing partners. The thought of caddying for him didn't enter my head. So when I saw him standing next to his clubs, talking with the starter, Kelly, I almost squealed like a girl. But I stifled it. I wasn't going to give him that satisfaction.

"How do you do, Mr. Woods," I said. "I'm Lainey and I'll be your caddie today. Do you mind if I call you 'Tiger?'"

He played along by shaking my hand. "By all means. Woods is my last name but Tiger is just my nickname. My real name is Deep."

"Your first name is Deep?"

"Yes," he said. "Deep N. D. Woods."

I groaned and Bushmills chuckled. Kelly almost lost it but got herself together and delivered her fast-and-smooth speech to the two newcomers. Bushmills shook their hands and deftly slung a bag strap over each shoulder.

While waiting for the fairway to clear, the golfers took a few warm-up swings and I eyed Travis with suspicion. When he looked up, he winked at me.

"Okay, funny guy. Are you gonna tell me what this is all about, or do I have to pretend-flirt with you all day like I do with regular guests?"

"I was hoping this would be a nice surprise," he said, putting his driver down. "After working such long hours lately, Andy gave me the day off. He said he'd work with Marco today and they could manage without me. I felt bad after cutting it short last night and I wanted to make it up to you."

He put an arm around me and whispered into my ear. "You can still pretend-flirt with me if you want to. Might be fun."

"I might, if it means you'll tip big."

As a matter of fact, it was a lot of fun. Hemlock Hollows, my favorite course because of its winding, natural routes from tees to greens, was the perfect loop for me to caddie with Travis. He played a good game, even allowing me to carry the bag and do all of my regular duties. Meanwhile, he explained why he thought the designers chose which direction to take and how they used the landscape to form the course layout. His excitement in imagining their creative process transferred to me and had me seeing this familiar course in a new way.

I remembered the Hollows from another day, caddying for Grant for the first time, and how pleased I had been with myself in presenting *my* course. He had disarmed me with his sweet nature and his respectful consideration for me, not to mention his good looks. For a headstrong and lonely girl with an uncertain future, it was a love affair to die for. But not really to change dreams for.

How I felt about Travis was different than anything I'd ever felt before. I understood, without any reservation, that what we had was honest-to-god real, everlasting love. Our dreams were a match.

Thinking about that, and loving every minute of our round together, kept all other thoughts out of my head.

Chapter 31

HE KISSED ME goodbye at precisely 4:49, according to the dashboard clock. We had had just enough time to run into town for a quick deli sandwich, then Travis brought me back to the caddie parking lot. I wanted to walk with the rest of the caddies as they were leaving from either the shack or from their cars, all of us doing our best to look uninterested.

I thought I spotted Tiny Sue's car, but in the mix of white jumpsuits and unrecognizable, street-clothed figures moving towards Madrone Hall, I couldn't be sure. Once inside the massive room I had to show some guts if I wanted a seat, and I did. The front three rows were empty, and a cluster of too-cool guys were standing near the doors ready to bolt at the first sign of a reprieve. I sat in the first chair of the third row and Tucson Johnny followed to sit next to me.

"So, here we are," he said in a low voice. "All is about to be revealed."

I nodded, but was dumbstruck by what I saw on the dais in front of us. Standing to the side of a podium, in a private confab with the general manager, were Larson and Tiny Sue.

Tucson Johnny muttered something that sounded like "wowza me yowza," which was better than anything I could come up with. A few more caddies got brave enough to fill up more seats as the GM moved to the podium and switched on the microphone. He tapped it twice and 200-plus caddies stopped talking.

He cleared his throat, then said, "Okay, let's get started. If we haven't yet had the opportunity to meet, I am Paul Smith, otherwise known as Smitty. As general manager of Singing Bluffs Resort, it's my job to direct all club operations, a big part of which is supervision of staff. It is a top priority with me to ensure guests receive exceptional service."

He paused, taking a slow methodical sweep of his audience.

"Understand, that is not just a glib, corporate slogan that I use to bullshit folks, particularly not those I count on to provide that exceptional service."

He spoke with a direct, homespun intensity that I, for one, did not doubt. He was an attractive man, with short, silver hair framing a pleasant face that had its share of hard-earned sun damage. I felt my anxieties diminishing the more he talked.

"The reason I've asked you all to come to this meeting is to draw your attention to that objective. Caddies are the backbone of a walking-only course. Your skills and behaviors set the tone for each and every golfer who asks for your services and expects a memorable round. I'm proud of our caddie corps and the continued expertise that has been available to our guests since Singing Bluffs first opened."

His head swiveled to address the whole room, ending up looking at Larson and Tiny Sue, who stood at his side and slightly behind. Their postures were at ease, their faces composed. I thought I saw Tiny Sue looking straight at me. The corners of her mouth curled up for a moment before turning back to Smitty.

"I've read the rating cards and I've witnessed firsthand some of our players' appreciation of their caddies. I wish I could be there more often. But there's a gap between what you do and what I do. I can't be everywhere. That's where the director of caddie services comes in. I need that staff member to put my vision of excellent customer service into play. It's a job with a lot of moving parts, and it takes someone with not only exceptional organizational skills, but with an unwavering integrity. That's why I've appointed Corey Larson as the new director of caddie services at Singing Bluffs Resort."

A roar of cheers came from his audience. Those of us with chairs got up out of them, applauding and whooping like crazy. The guys standing in the back and on the edges jostled each other in their exuberance. Larson grinned like I'd never seen before. Tiny Sue clapped along with us. Then Smitty stood aside to give Larson the mic.

Larson had to withstand a barrage of shouted gibes from the smartasses in the crowd, which he looked embarrassed about. But eventually he said, "Thank you, everybody. Now shut up a minute. I've got something to say. I want to publicly thank Smitty for giving me this opportunity and having the trust that I can do the job. I believe I can, with the help of all the management staff that keep this place running, and all of you."

Applause broke out again, then Smitty stepped up and held his hand out for silence.

"I know you'll do a great job, Corey, and you will have our help. To that end, you're going to need a new caddie master."

I looked at Tiny Sue standing there motionless. She was definitely looking right back at me. I got chills, and I heard Tucson Johnny whisper, "Hot damn." At the end of the row, against the wall, I saw Bushmills standing with Jake and Lyle. All three of them wore grins and held their hands in front of them ready for some supersize clapping.

Smitty said, "Ms. Bunnell, would you step forward please?"

She did, shook Smitty's hand, and looked everywhere but at the expectant onlookers in front of her.

"You all know Sue Bunnell here," Smitty continued, "and know that she's been an outstanding caddie with us since the beginning. Now she'll be taking Mr. Larson's position in the caddie facility."

The anticipated applause was delivered, and I felt like my face would break apart and my hands would fall off by the time we stopped. Tiny Sue now presented her slim, short stature, with her perfectly-coiffed hair and manicured nails, to her crew with an air of confidence.

Smitty dropped the handshake and addressed us again. "Now you might think that managing tee sheets is all there is to wrangling loopers, but you'd be wrong. Does anyone here remember signing something called 'The Caddie Handbook and Service Agreement?' Probably not."

That got a big laugh. He went on. "That document serves as *the* contract between caddies and management, the signed agreement between the two parties. Well, I owe you all an apology. It's been brought to my attention, by Sue here and a couple of others..."

He scanned the audience as if searching for those whistle-blowers.

"...that our handbook is a load of crap."

More laughter. But not from me. My anxieties were starting to act up again.

"I'm leaving it to Corey and Sue to draft a new set of guidelines for you and all other caddies joining us this season, and I will rely on them to help me enforce it. We want a handbook that clarifies and emphasizes the spirit of Singing Bluffs that we want to show the golf world. I'm ashamed to admit that we've let things slip in that regard. We've gotten sloppy in upholding the standard to which everyone who works here should be held. I mean to hold that standard high again and make this resort a place with some real class, a resort Eden Beach is proud to claim, a resort where *everyone* is treated with respect."

He paused but did not look away from the crowd of caddies, some seated, some standing, who waited for his next words.

"I'm not just talking about how you're expected to treat guests, but about how *you shall be treated* by everyone employed here at Singing Bluffs." His body rose higher behind the podium, demanding our full attention in case he hadn't gotten it already.

"I make this a promise. I will see to it that each of you, no matter what size, shape, or color you come in, will be given the respect and dignity your profession deserves."

At that, the whole audience stood and applauded without hoots and hollers. I was so proud of them. And of myself.

Chapter 32

SMITTY DISMISSED US after a brief thank-you for our attention and for being such "remarkable ambassadors of the resort." At any other time, I would've thought that was carrying things a bit far, but after hearing his praise the mood in the room was that of the totally worthy. Judging by the comments I heard from the beaming baggers leaving the hall, they might have been heading for the next flight to St. Andrews.

I tried to get to Tiny Sue to congratulate her, but some long-legged well-wishers beat me to it. Bushmills was there, of course, and so were Jake, Johnny, Lyle, A.J., even Spider. They and other senior caddies had formed a loose line, putting a hand out to either Tiny Sue, Larson, or Smitty before leaving. There was a formality to the scene that I understood to be an unwritten rule of professional courtesy. It was how people treat people, like golfers shaking our hands before and after a round. These were contracted workers showing respect for their managers, and vice versa.

A couple other first-years besides me were starting to get the idea. Cheech and the two guys I'd seen the other day on the putting green stood behind me as we waited our turn to thank the GM and congratulate Larson. When I finally got close to Tiny Sue, she threw both arms around me.

"Lainey! See? I told you it wasn't going to be a bad thing."

I hugged her back and we jumped a little bit, kinda doing a happy dance.

"Hey, hey, hey," Cheech said, "There'll be no jumping up and down and squealing like little girls. That's our caddie master you're hugging, you know."

I glanced at our GM to see what kind of reaction he showed, and he smiled back at me. I looked away with embarrassment.

"I haven't started the job yet, Cheech," Tiny Sue said, "so I'm allowed. Come here you big oaf."

She got Cheech in a head lock, which wasn't easy with their height difference, and knuckled the top of his head. He yelled, then backed away with a red face.

He called out, "Hey, Mr. Larson, is she allowed to give us noogies?"

Larson held a deadpan face before answering. "That's something we'll have to address in the caddie handbook, but my first inclination is to say, 'only when needed.'"

Cheech and the others groaned. Then Tiny Sue laughed and gave him a pat on the shoulder. "Nah, it's not needed. I'm sorry, Cheech. I'm just excited. After tonight, no more noogies. I vow to run the shack in much the same way

Larson did. But tonight, I'm having my last fling as one of the squad."

She hooked her arm in mine and walked me toward the nearest door.

"And since it may be my last chance to drink as just another looper, I'm buying the house a round at Pappy's."

We beat the rush for the door, and I took a quick look back. It was hard to believe the high spirits everyone was in. Smitty was joking around with Bushmills, Larson actually laughed at something Tucson Johnny said. We would never have seen this kind of thing with Art in the picture.

The crowd thinned as we walked towards the parking lot and I finally got to say what I'd been thinking since Smitty made the announcement.

"You did good, Sue. I am really happy for you. I know you'll be the best caddie master ever, and I..."

"Oh stop. Lainey, I wouldn't even be here if it weren't for you."

"Why do you say that? I didn't do anything."

"Only got the whole ball rolling, that's all. If it hadn't been for your stubborn resistance to leaving this place, I would never have come back. You got me thinking about how I should stick it out and help make things better instead of running off. And it was your perseverance and your honesty in talking with that writer that opened things up, got everyone thinking."

"I'm not too sure everyone was thinking nice thoughts, though."

"Ha. You mean like Miami?" she asked.

"Yeah, Miami."

"Well, you'll never guess who the first one out the door was after Smitty introduced me."

"You're kidding. What a jackass. Do you think he'll leave for good? Can't handle taking direction from a girl?" The thought made me smile.

"If he can't then he'd better go, otherwise he'll have plenty of primping time in the caddie shack."

We were at Sue's car, and she turned to me before getting in.

"Lainey, I'm gonna need more of your help. There's bound to be more guys like Miami that won't be thrilled that I got Larson's position. Will you promise to back me up when they start giving me a hard time? You can tell me in private if I'm doing something stupid, but in front of the guys will you stand by me?"

"Hell, Sue. You know I will. You're my mentor."

"No, I'm not. I'm your teammate." She got in her car and held her clenched fist high out the window as she pulled away.

I returned the salute and we yelled in chorus, "Power to the Short Grrrls!"

WE'D MISSED HAPPY hour, but the clientele didn't seem to care what the clock said or that their drinks were costing more. The only one not showing her happy face was Jessica. She had been kept on after her normal shift ended to help Curly. He was behind the bar, and Jessica was taking trays of drinks to the tables.

"Hey, Jess. Some crowd, huh?" I said as she slid by.

She shot me a murderous glare and muttered, "I hate caddies."

She was right. Over seventy-five percent of the people there were caddies, some still in their jumpsuits. I thought that some of them didn't really give a rat's ass who was running the caddie services at their resort. The fact that they had survived a mandatory meeting was reason enough to party.

I tried to make my way through the crush without bumping against people, but it was impossible. No matter how I contorted my body, the boobs came into contact with the body of someone else. At one point, I was jostled from behind and the boobs smashed into the white-clad back of one of those someones, unfortunately not one I recognized.

"Whoa there, honey," the guy said when he turned around. "You oughta watch where you're pointin' those things."

His friends laughed and he advanced even further so that our fronts were closer together.

"Sorry." I ducked and tried to keep moving.

"Wait a minute," he said, his eyes never leaving my chest, "what's your hurry? The least you can do after assaulting me like that is let me buy you a drink."

"No, thank you. I'm trying to find somebody."

He blocked me again and said, "Well, you found me. Aren't I good enough?"

There was a glimmer of cognition when he finally looked up. "You're that uppity caddie chick, aren't you? You got somethin' against men? Is that it?"

"Fuck off, douchebag. She's just trying to get through."

A hand latched onto my elbow and I turned to see Rocks standing there, squaring off against the douchebag. He had his backup man, Corky, right behind him, and it looked like that was enough to level the playing field. The rowdies made like it was all a joke and we slipped passed them.

When we got to a clearing, Rocks let go of my arm and avoided my eyes.

"Thanks, Rocks. That was so sweet, what you just did." That got his attention. "What's the deal? You're like a decent human being all of a sudden."

He snorted, then gave me his normal, sleazy smile. "You wish." He elbowed Corky and turned to go. "I'm still gonna call you Tit-swell."

"And you'll always be Rocksy the Rake to me," I said to his back.

I found Twitch at his usual barstool, almost buried behind a wall of more rough-talking loopers.

"You okay back there, Twitch?"

"Yeah, sure, Lainey. Come here, take my seat."

"No, no. Really, Twitch. I'd rather stand. I'm still kind of wound-up."

"So, I gather, are these boys." He indicated the whole room with his miniscule head bob. "Sue was just here a minute ago. I offered her a seat but she went to the back somewhere. I think she's still here, though."

"Yeah, I'm sure she's still here. But I've talked to her already."

Curly set a beer down in front of me, saying, "Tiny Sue got this," before hurrying off.

Twitch watched me take a big drink, chuckling to himself.

"What? What's funny?"

"Well, I've already heard all about what happened. These boys have been talking since they came in about what Paul Smith had to say, and I was just wondering, Lainey. Are you going to stop worrying now about what trouble you *might* be in?"

I grinned at the old dude, feeling pretty special that I had someone like him looking out for me. "I might. Do you think I'll be okay for a while?"

He chuckled some more and, nodding, said, "You're going to be okay, Lainey. You're going to be fine." He took a sip of his beer and set it down again. "By the way, if you're looking for Travis, he's sitting right back there."

"Oh yeah? I didn't see him. Where is he?"

"He's in the back booth," Twitch said. He turned back to the bar and was looking straight ahead, but I saw his mouth curl into a little smile. "He's been there quite a while, talking with Brian and Frank. You know, those two realtor fellas."

Chapter 33

TRAVIS STOOD WHEN he saw me coming. "Hi, babe," he said, shyly wrapping an arm around my waist.

I didn't get a kiss but I said hi, anyway.

"You know Brian and Frank?"

Brian answered before I could. "Oh, yeah. Lainey was our 'group caddie' at Hemlock Hollows. Remember that? You had to escort us even though we had pushcarts."

"Yeah. How's it going, guys? I hear you've been keeping Travis company while I was at the meeting."

Frank nodded. He looked a little glassy-eyed and I noticed empty highball glasses on the table that Jess hadn't cleared yet. "As a matter of fact, we were just talking about you," he said.

There was an instant reaction from Travis and Brian that I couldn't exactly read, but I could tell that Frank wasn't supposed to say that.

"Oh, yeah? What about?"

Brian got out of his chair, held it out for me, and said, "Just that we thought you were a good caddie. You really showed us a thing or two. We should do it again sometime, whenever we get another chance to play at the Bluffs. Come on, Frank. We'd better get outa here."

Frank stood, none too gracefully, and said, "Travis, you give it some more thought...you know, what we talked about, and we'll follow up a little later." He gave me a look that could've been a smile. With some drunks, it's so hard to tell a smile from a leer.

"Let's go, Frank," Brian urged. "I'll call you, Trav."

When they'd gone, Travis and I pulled our chairs closer together and I finally got my hello kiss.

Then I asked, "So what was that all about? Are you cooking up something with these guys?"

"Umm, sort of, maybe. I'll tell you later. So, tell me all about the big meeting."

In the time it took us to finish our beers, I talked and he listened while we sat in our cozy corner, oblivious to the noise beyond us. Travis wanted all the juicy details and was the perfect audience. He appreciated my descriptions and got excited over the parts of the speeches that I got excited over. We were about to leave when Tiny Sue came over to our table. She held two extra bottles of Bud besides the one she was drinking.

Travis laughed at her. "Hey, you already bought us one. Remember? Or are you too plastered?"

"No, I'm not plastered, Smarty. I'm only on my second – it just looks worse because I've been talkin' so much."

She plopped herself onto a chair and sighed. "Phew! I'll be glad to not have to do this anymore."

"Do what?" I asked.

"Try to keep up with these alcoholic loopers. I'm more like the pace-yourself kind of social drinker. I think that's the more accepted style for a caddie master."

I asked, "Can I still drink with you once in a while if I don't cramp your style?"

"You, Lainey, are not an alcoholic looper. I can keep up with you."

"In that case," Travis said, and picked up a bottle.

"Hold up, Travis," Tiny Sue said. "I want to make a toast."

She handed me the remaining bottle and we held them out, ready to clink. She smiled at me and said, "Here's to the next, and greatest, Senior Caddie at Singing Bluffs Resort."

I started laughing. Travis looked puzzled, like he wasn't sure what the joke was.

"It's a little early for that, Sue, but I'll drink to it anyway," I said.

"It's no joke, Lainey. Larson told me today. He's not going to wait until the High Season Caddie Party like usual. He said he wants to give the honors to those who deserve it now, before the seasonal caddies get back. Art always made a big show of rewarding his posse of delinquents, holding the Senior Caddie pins hostage until the resident first-years kissed his ass. Larson's changing that."

I sat stunned until Travis put his arm around me.

"Congratulations, Wonder Woman. You're a full-fledged, three-day-weekenders' *assigned caddie* now."

We drank, but I was still too shocked to put words together. I finally managed, "How...I mean...who...?"

"The only ones he mentioned were you, Cheech, Long Johns, and Rocks."

That Rocks and I made it out of the bucket at the same time made me smile.

"I know, right? Larson said Rocks had worked hard this winter and was a good example to other slackers. Go figure. Who am I to judge?" Tiny Sue shrugged. "He's going to make the announcement and hand out pins tomorrow morning, before first tee times. So you'd better be there early, girl. No staying in bed late with this guy."

The guy she pointed to snuggled next to me with a shit-eating grin on his adorable face.

"Well then," I said, "we'd better not waste any time. Drink up."

"WE SHOULD MAKE this our version of smoking a cigarette after making love here."

"Sounds good," Travis said. "Except it might be a little chilly in the dead of November."

We were sitting on the bench he'd built, wrapped together in a down comforter, Rover lying at our feet. It was a warm night, frogs were making their music–a good sign that another spring rain was coming. But above us, the cloudless and moonless sky at the cabin was full of stars.

"Maybe," I said.

"Maybe what?"

"Maybe it will be too chilly to sit out here in November. Aren't you paying attention?"

"Sorry. I was...distracted."

"Well, I think even if it's cold, I'll still want to be here on your porch and look at the night sky." I held his face in my hands and kissed him. "Hey, you don't have your glasses on. How can you see the stars without your glasses? Do you want me to go get them for you?"

I made an attempt to get up but he pulled me back.

"No, Lainey, please sit down."

"Uh, oh. You called me 'Lainey.'"

"The reason I didn't put my glasses back on is...is because I'm not sure I want to see your face when I tell you this."

My insides lurched. My eyes started stinging and no matter how much I blinked it didn't help.

I blurted, "Tell me what?"

He grasped my hand and looked at it, not at my face.

"I know you love this cabin, and I do, too. But what if...what if this wasn't where I lived?"

I was about to explode. Before that inevitability, though, he stepped up his pace.

"I mean, what if we sat on the porch of a real house, somewhere close to Eden Beach, a new house of our own? Of *our* own. It wouldn't be brand new, of course, or huge, or maybe even it'll be almost a tear-down. But with property, where we could eventually build a home that's exactly what we want. And we'd have room to raise stuff, like vegetables, or flowers, or our own beef. Whatever you want."

He finally looked up at me. He was doing a fairly good job of holding it together. But even more surprising, so was I.

We took a quiet breath or two. Then I said, "You're saying we should buy property. Together. And live together."

He bit his lower lip. "That's what I'm saying." Getting his second wind, he added, "I've got Brian and Frank looking for property. That's what we were doing earlier. But we need to talk to them together so they know what *we* are looking for. If there is a *we*."

"Okay," I said, taking my time, "let's say there is a *we*. How does this work?"

Getting excited now, Travis said, "I've talked to the bank and, thanks to Andy and the guarantee that I'll be the course superintendent when Azalea Leas opens next summer, they like my business plan. I can get a mortgage. And now that you're a senior caddie, you'll be working more. With both of us having dependable income, it will be that much easier."

At that moment my gut was seizing but my brain was amazingly calm.

"I don't want to push you into anything, Lainey, please believe that..."

"I do believe you."

"...because I just want you with me. I want you to be with me forever." He grabbed both my hands and held them to his lips. "I love you. That's all I can say."

I tried to look into his eyes, but mine were watering so much my vision was probably as blurred as his. Without unclasping our hands, I used the back of his hand to wipe the drips.

"I love you, too. And I love that you've..."

"Wait. I'm not finished. I have to say that you don't have to agree to anything yet. Just think about it, seriously, for as long as it takes. I'm not going to rush you. I'll wait."

We stopped talking and listened to the frogs for a moment. A long moment. I knew my answer, as well as I knew that I loved him more than anything. I wouldn't tell him, though. I had to think about it, like he said.

It was true. Things really do fall into place, just like everyone told me they would.

Travis, still holding my hands against his lips and looking into my eyes, whispered, "I can't tell. Are you smiling?"

"Yes."

~